DEADLY INFERNO!

Clint picked up a burning piece of wood, grabbed a handful of hay, and carried them to one of the walls. He set the hay down at its base, then touched the burning wood to it. It flared and burned as if the fire was hungry and the wall was its food.

Suddenly the entire wall was burning, and the heat was becoming oppressive. The wall was billowing smoke, which would soon fill the interior of the stable.

In his effort to escape, he just might have sealed his own death warrant . . .

*　　*　　*

SPECIAL PREVIEW!

Turn to the back of this book for a sneak-peek excerpt from the exciting, brand new western series . . .

FURY

. . . the blazing story of a gunfighting legend.

Also in THE GUNSMITH series

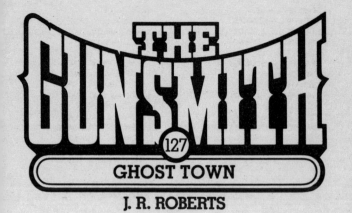

THE GUNSMITH

127

GHOST TOWN

J. R. ROBERTS

JOVE BOOKS, NEW YORK

GHOST TOWN

A Jove Book / published by arrangement with
the author

PRINTING HISTORY
Jove edition / July 1992

ISBN: 0-515-10882-0

Jove Books are published by The Berkley Publishing Group,
200 Madison Avenue, New York, New York 10016.
The name "JOVE" and the "J" logo
are trademarks belonging to Jove Publications, Inc.

PRINTED IN THE UNITED STATES OF AMERICA

10   9   8   7   6   5   4   3   2   1

PROLOGUE

The letter sent to Clint Adams, in Labyrinth, Texas, was sent by someone who knew him. Someone who knew that a call for help from a friend would never be ignored. Someone who knew that Labyrinth was virtually a mailing address for Clint Adams, who spent much of his time traveling.

It was sent by someone who had not seen Clint Adams in some time and was very anxious to renew acquaintances.

It arrived in Labyrinth with no return address, and it was not signed. The tone of the letter suggested that a friend had written it:

Dear Clint:
Need your help very badly. You're the only one who can help me. Please meet me in Patience, Oklahoma, on the 24th of August. I will explain everything then. I know I can count on you to be there.

Clint finished reading the letter and passed it across the table to Rick Hartman. They were sitting in Rick's Place, Hartman's saloon. It was noon, and there were very few patrons present.

1

"What do you think?" Rick asked after he'd read it.

"That's my line," Clint said. "What do *you* think about it?"

"From the tone of it, I'd say a friend needed your help pretty badly."

Rick handed the letter back.

"Why isn't it signed?"

Rick shrugged. "Maybe whoever wrote it forgot to sign it. It sounds like it was written quickly, and under stress."

"Maybe," Clint said, scanning it again. "It doesn't sound like anyone I know."

"Have you ever been to Patience, Oklahoma?"

"No."

"Have you ever heard of Patience, Oklahoma?"

"No."

"So there's no clue there. What's the letter smell like?"

"What?"

Rick took it back and sniffed it.

"No perfume. Probably wasn't written by a woman. If it was she would have left *some* scent on it."

Clint took the letter back and said, "What are you, a detective?"

"Just common sense," Rick said. "Women leave a scent behind, or hadn't you ever noticed?"

Clint realized that Rick was right. He had known enough women to know that, even fresh from a bath, they each had a special scent all their own.

"Okay," he said, "okay, let's say it's a man. Who is it?"

"My friend," Rick said, "with the amount of traveling you've done over the years, and the number of people you've met and befriended, it could be anyone."

"Some detective."

"There's something else to consider."

"What?"

"With all the traveling you've done, you've also made a lot of enemies."

"You think this is a trap of some sort?"

Rick shrugged. "It's a thought."

Clint fell silent and scanned the letter again.

"Well," he said, finally, "I guess there's only one way to find out."

"You're going to go?"

"How else do I find out who it is?"

"Ignore the letter."

"What?"

"Ignore it," Rick said again. "Maybe they'll write again, and sign it next time."

"But on August twenty-fourth this person is going to be in Patience, Oklahoma."

"And you won't," Rick said. "Maybe he'll go from there to the nearest town with a telegraph, if Patience doesn't have one."

"And maybe whatever trouble he's in will catch up to him before that."

"So you're gonna go save him?"

"We've gone round and round with this before, Rick," Clint said.

"I know."

Rick had often tried to break Clint of the habit of rushing to people's aid, whether they asked for it or not. He had been unsuccessful.

"So go, but take somebody with you."

"Like you?"

Rick shook his head.

"I'm not curious enough to make the trip," Rick said, "and that, my friend, is the basic difference between you and me."

"That," Clint said, standing up, "and my success with women."

He headed for the door while Rick sputtered, trying to think of an appropriate response.

ONE

He felt the impact even before he heard the shot. In fact, his head was ringing too loudly for him to hear the shot clearly. All he really knew was that he was falling from the saddle and that pain was flashing through his head. He hit the ground hard, and instinctively started rolling to avoid any additional shots. He came to a stop with his back against a horse trough but with his gun in his hand.

It was quiet.

He stayed where he was, trying to piece things back together. He had such a headache he couldn't think straight. He lifted his left hand to his head, and his fingers came away bloody. He didn't have time to investigate the severity of the wound. He had to get off the street before the shooting started again.

Just then, the shooting started again.

The lead started kicking up dust near his feet, and he scrambled away from the trough, staggering to his feet. He started running left, but lead started smacking into the ground in front of him. He reversed direction and started running again. He had gone about twenty feet when lead started landing in front of him again. He looked to his left and saw that he was standing in front of a saloon. He charged through the batwing doors, and one of them went flying from the impact.

Inside he paused to look around, but when a window shattered and bullets started flying into the place, he hit the floor, turning a table over for cover. He could hear the lead chewing up the table he was behind. Given enough time, it would eat through the wood. He needed thicker cover. He needed someplace he could lay low long enough to make some sense out of what was happening.

He looked around, spotted the bar, and decided to make for it when the shooter had to reload. The shooting went on for so long he thought there had to be more than one shooter. Either that, or the guy had an arsenal.

Finally the shooting stopped. Clint counted to three, then ran for the bar. He made it without any shots being fired. He sat down on the floor with his back to the bar and tried to catch his breath. He felt for the head wound again and found that the bullet had creased his skull right at the hairline. He looked around and found a rag under the bar. It was filthy, but it would have to do. He grabbed a bottle of whiskey, poured some on the rag, and tried to clean the wound as best he could. The whiskey burned, but oddly enough, it seemed to clear his head a bit. He tied the rag around his head to control the bleeding, then settled back to reconstruct what had happened. . . .

In response to the letter he had received in Labyrinth, Texas, Clint came to Patience, Oklahoma. When he came within sight of the town it struck him that the place was very serene-looking. As he got closer, he could see that it was not serene—it was deserted, and had been for some time.

Patience was a ghost town.

He had ridden into town down the main street, look-ing for any sign of life. The only sign he found was when someone started shooting at him. . . .

Well, there wasn't much to reconstruct. All he had done was ride in, and someone had shot him. Now that he thought about it, he realized that the shooting was carefully planned to happen where it did. All those shots that had landed at his feet had been expertly placed to herd him into this saloon.

Rick Hartman had been right. The letter, the plea for him to come to Patience, Oklahoma, *had* been a trap— but a trap to do what? It was perfectly clear that the shooter could have killed him at any time. But why just wound him? Why drive him into this saloon?

And when would he get the answers to these ques-tions?

TWO

"Hey, out there!" Clint shouted.

There was no answer.

Clint risked standing up, and a shot was immediately fired. It whizzed past his head and struck the dirty mirror behind the bar, shattering a portion of it.

Clint ducked back down. It remained obvious that the shooter didn't want to kill him yet, but there was no point in tempting him.

He looked at the point where the bullet had struck the mirror. With that, and the other shots, Clint figured that the shooter was in another building across the way, on ground level. The initial shots—the one that wounded him, and those that followed immediately— might have come from a rooftop, but all of those fired into the saloon came from ground level. The shooter could clearly see the interior of the saloon from where he—or they—were. He was effectively pinned down behind the bar. What he had considered to be his best cover was turning out to be his prison.

Rick Hartman had been right about something else: over the years Clint Adams had made a lot of enemies. Now one of them was out there. The intentions of the shooter had to be to kill him eventually, but the shooter probably wanted him to suffer first, to think about what was happening. Whoever was out there probably wanted him to do exactly what he was doing right now—racking his brain to try to figure out who it was who was out there.

Across the street the shooter began to reload the three rifles that were leaning against the wall next to the window. There were also three pistols lying on the store counter next to the window. The shooting, as far as the shooter was concerned, was now concluded—for a while. Now it was time to give Clint Adams time to search his memory and to study his prison. He would find that there was no way out of the saloon save by the front door. Given that fact, he would have no choice but to try to figure out who was shooting at him. The shooter would give him ample time to do so.

Of course, Adams would never be able to identify the shooter correctly, but he would wear himself out mentally trying. His wound—a carefully placed wound, and a calculated risk by the shooter—would wear him out physically as well. Once he was mentally and physically worn ragged, the shooter would march across the street and finish the job.

THREE

Carefully, Clint once again lifted his head above the bar. The movement brought no gunfire. Bolder still, he stood up. When that did not bring gunfire, he walked out from behind the bar.

"Letting me examine my prison, eh?" he said to himself. "Well, thank you very much."

Clint decided to take full advantage of his jailer's benevolence. First he inspected the room he was in. The saloon was a small one, probably the town's second, and it had only one floor. That was probably why his jailer had picked it. He wouldn't have two floors to cover from across the street.

There was a doorway in the back wall, but no door. He walked to it and found himself in a short hallway that led to a door. It was probably the back door to the saloon. He tried it, but it wouldn't budge. He put his shoulder to it, but to no avail. He drew back and kicked it but made no progress. If it were simply locked, it would have moved. Therefore he came to the conclusion that it was somehow nailed shut.

His exertions had weakened him and he leaned against the wall, hoping he would not faint. Using the wall for balance, he made his way back to the main room of the saloon. There was no other way out, then, but by the front doors or windows. There were no other windows, the rear door was sealed to him, and there were no other rooms.

His jailer had picked his prison well. To have trapped him in a larger building would have made it harder to keep him inside.

Still feeling dizzy, he went back around behind the bar and sat on the floor. The whiskey bottle he had used to clean his wound was still there, so he lifted it to his lips and drank. The burning sensation it left as it went down seemed to clear his mind. Suddenly he thought about Duke. Where had the big gelding gotten to? He wondered if he had come to any harm.

All he *could* do was wonder, for there was nothing he could do for Duke even if he was hurt. There was precious little he could do for himself, too.

Precious little . . .

Annie Martin looked to be eighteen years old or so, but Clint could tell by looking at her that she was an "advanced" eighteen or so. It wasn't only the woman's body that was barely concealed by her simple dress, it also was the look in her eyes when she looked at him.

She had blond hair that was almost white, and eyebrows to match. Her skin, however, was tanned dark, and the contrast was striking. She lived with her grandfather on his farm, and from the looks of her hands, he worked her hard. She was, however, built for hard work. Her body was strong and sturdy, with firm, thrusting breasts, and powerful legs and buttocks. It made a man's hands itch just to look at her.

Clint stopped at the Martin farm to water his horses, and that's when he saw her, coming out of the stable. She stopped and watched as he approached. She stood with her right arm at her side, the other behind her back, but her left hand was gripping her right arm. Clint didn't think he could do that.

"Hello," he said.

"Howdy." She squinted up at him, one eye almost closed against the sun. "Can I help ya?"

"I'd like to water my horses, if I may," he said.

"Sure, go ahead."

He got down and walked his team to the trough, then went behind the rig and got Duke and led him to the water as well.

"That's a beautiful horse." Her tone echoed her admiration.

"Thanks."

"Must take a mighty strong man to ride him."

He smiled at her and said, "No, just me."

He pumped some fresh water into his cupped hand and sipped from it.

"I can get you a cup," she offered.

"No, I don't want to bother—"

"It ain't no bother," she said. "I'll be right back."

She walked to the house, and he watched her buttocks bunch and clench beneath her dress. If nothing else, this was a healthy girl.

She came back out of the house and handed him a tin cup.

"Thank you," he said. He pumped water into it and drank deeply.

"Where you heading?" she asked.

"Nowhere in particular," he told her. "Just traveling."

"I wish I could do that," she said. "I ain't never been away from hereabouts." Her tone was regretful.

He looked around and could see why she sounded so mournful. The ground looked like packed, hard dirt, and the house and barn were falling into disrepair.

"You don't live here alone, do you?" he asked.

"Naw," she said, "I live with my grandpa . . . but he ain't here now."

"He left you alone?"

"He had to go to Gallup."

"Where's that?"

" 'Bout a day's ride due east," she said. "It's the county seat. He had business there. Left this morning. Won't be back until at least day after tomorrow, maybe more. He's got a woman he sees in Gallup, and he'll probably get likkered up, too."

"A woman? Your grandpa?"

"Well . . ." she said sheepishly, "actually, he gets hisself a whore."

"How old is your grandpa?"

"Sixty, or thereabouts. He's real . . . spry, though."

"I guess so."

She looked at the sky and said, "It's gonna be dark soon. You'll never make the next town."

"I'll be all right."

She gave him a baleful look and said, "Tell you the truth, the first day Grandpa is away I always get a little . . . nervous."

"I see."

"You could sleep in the barn, if you like."

"Well—"

"It would give your animals a little extra rest."

She was right about that. He looked at the sky. She was right, too, about it being dark soon.

"There's plenty of hay," she said. "You'd be real comfortable."

He smiled at her and said, "You talked me into it."

"I could make you somethin' to eat," she said. "All's we got is some beans and bacon. Grandpa'll be bringin' back some supplies."

"Beans and bacon is fine."

She smiled, stuck out her hand, and said, "My name is Annie Martin."

He took her hand and shook it. She had a firmer grip than a lot of men he'd known.

"Clint Adams, Annie," he said, "and I thank you kindly for your hospitality."

"Clint," she said, "it's you who's doin' me a big favor."

He didn't find out just how big until later on.

FOUR

The beans and bacon were filling, although they weren't very tasty. Annie said that her grandpa usually did the cooking. Clint told her not to worry about it. As for the coffee, it was enough to say that Clint Adams, the world's most voracious coffee drinker, stopped after one cup.

After dinner Annie was cleaning the kitchen, and Clint told her that he was going to finish looking after his stock and then turn in. He explained that he wanted to get an early start in the morning. She thanked him for staying, saying that she felt safer knowing that he was out in the stable.

Clint left the house and made sure that Duke and the team were properly cared for, fed, and bedded down. After that he took a couple of blankets out of his rig and made a bed for himself on a hill of hay. He then made himself comfortable and fell asleep.

Sometime during the night he heard the barn door open. He was off the bed of hay as quietly and quickly as a cat, gun in hand. It was pitch dark, but it only took a few moments for his eyes to adjust. He saw a shape enter and move carefully through the dark. He assumed that the intruder could not see as well as he could, and that suited him just fine.

As the intruder moved deeper into the barn, Clint

stepped out behind the person and said, "That's far enough."

He didn't know what to expect, but it wasn't a woman's scream.

"Annie?" he said. "Wait a minute."

He found a lamp and lit it. Annie was standing stock-still, clad only in a man's threadbare robe, her shoulders hunched.

"Are you all right?" he asked her.

She was staring at his gun, and then looked at him and said, "You scared me half to death."

"I'm sorry," he said, lowering the gun. "I didn't expect you."

"You didn't?"

"No," he said. "Is something wrong?"

"No," she said, "I just get . . . lonely sometimes."

"Lonely?"

"There ain't never no one to talk to but Grandpa," she said. "I thought maybe we could . . . talk."

"Talk?"

"Yes."

In the middle of the night, he thought, but then she'd been so hospitable it wouldn't be right for him to turn her away.

"All right," he said, "we'll talk."

He walked to his haybed, put his gun back in his holster, and then lay on his side.

"What do you want to talk about?"

"I don't know," she said. "Maybe some of the places you been. Can I sit here?"

She perched on the edge of his haybed before he could say anything. The robe she was wearing had been worn so thin that it was obvious that she was wearing very little, if anything, beneath it. It rode up her legs, revealing strong, smooth calves and thighs. She left it that way. Neither did she do anything about the fact that it was gaping open in front enough to reveal the smooth slopes of her breasts. He could smell her hair, and her skin, and another scent, something more . . . primal.

I must be slowing down, he thought, realizing what she had come out there for—and it wasn't to talk.

He gave it some thought. She was probably of age, and the mixed scents she was giving off were certainly having their effect on him. He was already erect.

"Annie," he said, "what did you really come out here for?"

"I tole you," she said, "I'm lonely."

"But you didn't come to talk, did you?"

She lowered her eyes and said, "No."

He reached out and lifted her chin with his hand.

"Annie, are you a virgin?"

"No," she said, "but I only done it a few times." She looked at him then and said, "I done it with boys. I want to do it with a man."

He studied her for a few moments and then said, "Come here."

Before she moved closer to him she rode up on her knees and let the robe slide down her shoulders and arms.

"You been a lot of places, I bet," she said. "Do you think I'm pretty?"

Her breasts were large and rounded, with heavy undersides and large, russet-colored nipples. He reached out and hefted the left one, than ran his finger over the nipples, which had already hardened.

"I don't think you're pretty," he said. "You're beautiful. Come here."

She moved close to him then, and he could feel the heat from her body. The robe was still bunched around her waist. He untied the robe and discarded it completely. Naked to the waist himself, he gathered her into his arms so that her breasts were crushed against him, and he kissed her. She kept her lips rigid and he had to tell her to relax. He used his mouth to open hers, and let his tongue slide into her sweet mouth. The kiss went on for a long time, and when it ended she was breathless, and wide-eyed with wonder.

"I ain't never been kissed like that before."

He kissed her again, and this time her tongue invaded his mouth, darting about avidly. While she was discovering the wonders of kissing, he slid his hand down over her belly until he was able to touch her wetness. She started, as if struck by lightning, and pulled her mouth away from his.

"What—" she said.

"Lie on your back," he instructed her, and she did so without question or hesitation.

He ran his mouth over her big breasts, wetting the nipples with his tongue, then sucking on them and finally biting them. She moaned and squirmed about on the blanket. He straddled her, still working on her breasts with his mouth while his penis rubbed against her pubic hair. He spent a long time on her nipples, then worked his mouth down over her ribs and belly. Finally his mouth was nestled against the wetness behind the blond pubic hair, and he ran his tongue up and down her, tasting her. She gasped when his tongue touched her clit, and her hands came down to hold his head there, as if she were afraid that he was going to move it away from her. He wasn't, not until he was finished.

His tongue lashed at her clit while she moaned and

cried out, lifting her buttocks off the blanket. He slid his hand beneath her to cup her big, firm buttocks and held her up off the blanket while he sucked on her. He could feel her belly begin to tremble with the approaching explosion, and when it came, she literally screamed.

He lifted himself over her before the first sensations could fade, and then entered her, loving the way her heat and her wetness closed around him. She came again as he entered her, and then he slid his hands beneath her again and began taking her in long, slow strokes, building to his own climax as she cried out twice more, and finally he was ready. . . .

FIVE

He came awake with a start.

For one frightening moment he didn't know where he was. What was even more frightening, he didn't know *who* he was.

He looked around him at the interior of the run-down, deserted saloon, and it all came flooding back to him. The ambush, the flight into the saloon . . . Jesus, had he fallen asleep? And what a dream—only it hadn't been a dream. He couldn't remember when exactly it had happened, but it *had* happened. It could have been yesterday, on his way here, or six months ago, on his way somewhere else. No, it wasn't yesterday, because he'd had his rig with him. It must have been months— or years—ago.

He felt very hot and realized suddenly that he had a fever. That must have been why he'd fallen asleep. Great—that was all he needed, to be unconscious when his friend outside came in to kill him.

He needed water, but there was none to be had in the saloon. Maybe if he called out to his assailant and told him that he'd die without water he'd let him go out and get some. He could promise to go right back into the saloon—except that he knew that once he was out of the saloon, he *wouldn't* go back inside. That was what he really needed to do, get out of the saloon and

23

then they could play the kids' game "tag" throughout the ghost town. If he could only get out of the saloon, they'd be on more even grounds.

First, though, he had to get to his feet. He braced his hands and his heels against the floor and started to push himself to a standing position. He was halfway there when everything started going around in circles.

Wait, wait, wait, he told himself, not so fast. Ease back down. We don't want to black out, do we—

Bill Wallmann was there, but Bill Wallmann was dead. He remembered that. Wallmann, with something growing inside his head, had chosen to face the Gunsmith rather than a doctor's scalpel.

Clint remembered that Anne Archer was there, too. Anne, who with her partners Sandy Spillane and Katy Littlefeather, formed a formidable bounty-hunting team. On this occasion, however, they had decided that they needed help, and Clint Adams was the man to help them.

Clint had a very warm spot in his heart for Sandy and Katy, but his feelings for Anne were special. Even back then, however, he had to put off dealing with his feelings for Anne Archer until he'd dealt with Bill Wallmann, a man with a considerable reputation for handling a gun.

He was facing Wallmann in the street, trying to talk him out of forcing the confrontation between the two of them, but Wallmann wouldn't be put off.

"I'm going to kill you unless you kill me," he'd said.

"This isn't the way, Bill—"

"You can tell me that, Clint? How would you rather die? From a bullet, or from something unknown inside your head?"

"It doesn't have to be unknown."

"I ain't gonna let no doctor cut me!"

"Bill—"

"Forget it, Adams!" Wallmann snapped. "At least this way I'll have a question answered that I been wondering about a long time. Who's better, you or me?"

"Damn it, Bill, don't make me—"

"Now, Gunsmith!"

They drew.

The shots woke him up.

He sat totally still and listened. Were they in his dream, or were they real? He passed his hand over his face, and the hand came away soaked wet. He wiped it dry on his thigh. He could still feel the heat of the fever behind his eyes. If he was going to survive this he was going to have to be able to tell reality from dreams.

This time he managed to work his way to his feet without falling over. He looked around, but nothing in the saloon seemed to have been disturbed. He came to the conclusion that the shots that had brought him to his senses had been in his head.

How long was this going to go on? It was bad enough he had reality to deal with. Was his mind going to be constantly going back to the past?

Wait a minute, he told himself, leaning on the bar for support. Maybe that was what he *should* be doing, examining his past for the answer to who was out there. It had to be somebody with an old grudge to settle. There was no other reason for things to happen the way they did. A stranger who wanted to kill him would have done so with the first shot. Herding him in here, nailing the rear door shut, that all spoke of someone who knew him and was playing cat-and-mouse games with him.

Maybe that was why his mind had gone back twice already on its own. The first time it had been a simple encounter with a girl. No danger there, not unless her grandpa had come looking for him. He didn't think that likely.

The second time it had dredged up Bill Wallmann, but Wallmann was dead.

It was plain that if his mind was going to come up with the answer, it was going to need some help.

SIX

Clint had never before taken the time to consider how many enemies he had made over the years. It was not the kind of list a man made proudly. In making the list he had to go back in his mind to places like South America, London, England, and even Australia. He had been to all those places, and in every one he had been forced into difficult situations, in some of which he'd had to kill to get out alive.

Trying to make a list now, he noticed something else he was not proud of. Most of the people who were on the list were dead. It was the nature of his reputation. Many of the men he had come up against had been after his reputation. Consequently, it had been a case of kill or be killed, as it had been with Bill Wallmann, Kim Chang, Larry Crook, and countless others.

With Trey Hatcher, though, it had been different. Trey Hatcher had faced him in the streets of a Montana town, and had then thought better of it and walked away.

Could it be Hatcher out there, or someone else who had not seen it through the first time they met? Were they trying to make up now for lost time?

Suddenly he felt sleepy and dizzy. Holding on to the bar, he again lowered himself to the floor. He sat there, wishing his health was a hundred percent. He just couldn't concentrate for long periods of time. The damn head wound was taking a lot out of him. He hoped some kind of infection wasn't setting in. It shouldn't. He had washed it with whiskey. He touched his head, pressing and prodding, and he didn't think it hurt any more—or any *less*—than a head wound was supposed to hurt. It was just sapping him of his strength, and his concentration.

Maybe, if he just closed his eyes for a second . . .

"Don't close your eyes."

He opened his eyes and listened. Someone had said something . . . but who?

"Come on," the voice said, "we've been in worse spots than this before."

"Yeah?" Clint said. "Name one."

"Abilene," the voice said. "Remember Abilene? The whole town was against us there, but we came through."

"Yeah, Bill, but . . ." Clint started, then stopped as he realized who he was talking to.

"That's right, old friend," the voice said, "it's me. Come on, up on your feet. I'm over here."

Clint frowned, then braced his hands and feet and fought his way to a standing position. His frown deepened when he saw the man seated at the table. He had a deck of cards in his hands and looked like he was dealing out poker hands. Next to his elbow was a bottle of whiskey and a partially filled glass.

Clint squinted in an effort to see better, but the man's face, his entire appearance, did not change. The hair was long and flowing, the mustache well cared for. He could see that the man was wearing a red sash, with two pistol grips protruding.

"This can't be," Clint said. "You're dead."

"I sure am," Wild Bill Hickok said, "and you will be, too, if you don't snap out of it. Clint," Hickok said, looking right at him now, "this little ghost town could end up being your Deadwood."

Deadwood Gulch, in Dakota Territory. That was the town where Wild Bill Hickok had been killed by a coward's bullet in the back. Clint, having lost his best friend and been reminded of his own mortality at the same time, had sought refuge in a bottle. It had taken his friend Rick Hartman to pull him out of it. Also, he had taken a trip to Deadwood to try to purge his own personal devil.

But now Hickok was here, staring at him with a bemused smile on his face.

"Bill," Clint said, staring at his friend, "what are you doing here?"

Hickok started dealing solitaire.

"I don't know," he said, watching the cards. "You called me here, I guess."

"Me?"

"Well," Hickok said, spreading his hands, "I'm dead, ain't I? I didn't come here on my own."

Some years back Clint had heard rumors that Wild Bill Hickok—or his ghost—had been seen in Mexico. He'd gone down and checked it out and had found— and dealt with—an impostor.

What was he dealing with now—a ghost, or an impostor? Clint came around the bar and walked over to the table to examine the man more closely. Once he had done that, he was convinced that this was Hickok.

That meant he was dealing with a ghost.

"You're a ghost."

"There's no such thing as ghosts."

"Then how do you explain your presence here?"

Hickok looked up at Clint and said, "I don't have to explain it. You do."

"This is crazy."

"I guess you've got a problem here, huh?"

"Yeah, I've got a problem," Clint said. "There's somebody out there who wants to kill me, I don't know who he is, and I'm seeing ghosts."

"Well," Hickok said, smiling, "this is a ghost town."

SEVEN

Clint sat down at the table and looked across at Hickok—only Hickok wasn't there.

"Wait a minute," Clint said. "Let's take this slow. Bill was never here. It was a dream, but I'm over here now instead of behind the bar. That means I walked in my sleep?" He thought about it for a few moments and then said "Wait a minute" again. "I wasn't asleep, I was unconscious . . . and now I'm conscious, and talking to myself." He threw his hands up in the air. After all, who else was there to talk to?

He wondered what his assailant must have thought when he staggered across the room in his "sleep" and sat at the table. In fact, why had he been allowed to sit here? Surely he must now be in the sights of whoever was across the street.

He frowned and looked across the room. There was a window on either side of the batwing doors. He could see nothing through the broken panes, but he was sure he was in plain sight. Why else would he have been maneuvered into this saloon?

At any moment a fatal shot could be fired at him. He decided to vacate the table and get back behind the bar. He stood up carefully, slowly, so as not to prompt any shooting, and started to walk slowly to the bar. He stopped short when he saw something under the table. He bent over and picked it up. It was a card, but not any old card. It was the ace of spades.

Across the street, the shooter was smiling. He had watched as Clint walked to the table, and then had smiled with great satisfaction as he watched Clint Adams talk to an empty chair.

He hadn't expected it to happen quite this soon, but it looked like the Gunsmith was starting to lose his mind.

Clint sat behind the bar and examined the card in his hand. He remembered in his dream that Hickok had dropped a card. This card, however, had been on the floor for some time. It was dusty, dog-eared, and bent. He hadn't noticed it when he first entered the saloon—or maybe he had. Maybe subconsciously he had seen it, and perhaps that triggered the dream—or hallucination.

He decided to set the card aside and not dwell on it. Hickok's appearance was a dream, or a hallucination, brought upon by his head wound. Nothing more.

Oddly, since having the Hickok dream, Clint felt a little better. He was not as warm, and he did not feel as weak. Maybe now he'd be able to apply himself to the problem of who his assailant could be, by looking back into his past. . . .

EIGHT

There was the time he worked with Heck Thomas in Wyoming, where they became involved in a range war. He had been at odds with the Wyoming Stock Growers' Association, and a man named Preston Flint. Some of the men who worked for Flint had ended up dead, but when Clint left Tannerville, Wyoming, on the banks of the Powder River, Flint had still been alive. Could it be that Preston Flint had decided to send someone after Clint Adams, even after more than five years?

That was one consideration.

Also about five years ago Clint had gone to New York City to find out who was writing dime novels called *The Legend of the Gunsmith*. Upon arrival he discovered that a woman he had known and liked, J. T. Archer, had been killed. Ultimately, Clint found the killer, but he had also felt certain at that time that the killer worked for a politician named Boss Kelly. Kelly certainly was not above hiring a killer, and he had the money, but what motive could he have had for sending someone after Clint Adams after all this time?

Boss Kelly, he felt, was not a viable option.

Working for the Secret Service at the behest of his friend Jim West, Clint had succeeded in disbanding

something called The Fast Draw League. He'd had
the help of Sandy Spillane back then, who had left her
partners Anne Archer and Katy Littlefeather to find her
brother. Jason Sharp, a man he had known previously, had founded the League, and disappeared when it
was disbanded. Could it be Jason Sharp himself who
was across the street? Or someone he hired? Maybe a
member of a new Fast Draw League?

A possibility.

What about the Comforts? Old Sam Comfort and
his boys were dead, compliments of Clint and Katy
Littlefeather. Clint had to break Katy out of jail in
Firecreek, Wyoming, and then they had taken care of
the Comforts. What if there were more Comforts out
there somewhere?

A possibility.

A couple of years ago Clint had rushed to Denver
when his friend Talbot Roper was shot. He had ended
up in a hunt for some gold, working with Heck Thomas,
Fred Hammer, and Anne Archer. He'd also worked
with another special lady in his life, Pinkerton detective
Ellie Lennox, whom he had met years earlier in Denver.
Ellie had been pretty upset with him toward the end of
that particular adventure. Also, Clint had beaten a lot
of people to that gold. It was silly to suspect Ellie, but
what of all the other people who were looking for that
gold, either to keep it or to turn it in for the reward?
People like Jake Benteen, a bounty hunter Clint knew,
though not well. He was much better acquainted with
Lacy Blake, who had worked with Benteen for a while
as his partner. They were working as partners when
Clint first met them. They could still be working as

partners, for all he knew, but he couldn't in all honesty suspect them.

Clint's head was spinning, not from his injury but from his mental journey into the past. So many names, friends, enemies, lovers.

Lovers.

Jesus, what about women who might have taken their time together a little more seriously than he had? There were a handful of women he still carried feelings for. The lady bounty hunters he had known, surely: Sandy Spillane, Katy Littlefeather, Lacy Blake, he considered them all friends. As for Anne Archer, his feelings for her were something more than friendly. And then there was the Wyoming rancher Beverly Press.

Clint made sure he always stopped in to see Beverly when he was in Wyoming, and Ellie Lennox when he visited Denver. The others he either crossed paths with, or responded to calls for help from.

Then there was the red-haired Scarlet, who some called The Scarlet Gun.

He could not think of a woman who might hate him enough to have this done to him.

All the soul-searching and mental time travel had taken its toll on Clint. He now felt wrung out, and hoped that he'd be able to close his eyes without seeing Wild Bill Hickok again.

Later he would wish that Hickok *had* returned in his sleep.

NINE

"Clint?"

He heard the voice and opened his eyes. He thought he heard it the first time. The voice was so familiar that it immediately woke him up.

"Clint?"

No, he thought, it couldn't be.

"Come on, Clint, dear."

Frowning, he worked his way to his feet and leaned on the bar. At the table where Hickok had been sitting there was now someone else.

"Joanna?" he said.

She turned her head and smiled at him. It was Joanna Morgan, the only woman he had ever asked to marry him.

But she was dead, killed soon after his proposal, in Alaska.

"Hello, Clint," she said. "You're in trouble, aren't you?"

"Yes," he said, still staring. "A lot of trouble."

"Poor darling."

"Joanna . . ."

"Yes, dear?"

"You're dead."

She smiled and said, "I know."

"What are you doing here? How did you get here?"

"Well," she said, "there you were, thinking of all your women, and you never once thought of me."

"Joanna," he said, "I always think of you. I was just . . . thinking of the women who were . . . alive."

"Because I'm dead, Clint," she said, "does that mean you love me less?"

He'd forgotten how beautiful she was. Her red hair had a luster that was almost unmatched. The only other woman he had ever seen who had hair like that was Anne Archer, and maybe Scarlet.

"You're thinking about some of your other women."

He started, embarrassed.

"I—"

"I don't hold that against you, darling," she said. "After all, I *am* dead. . . ."

He woke with a start. He stood up too quickly to look at the table, and had to hold on while a dizzy spell passed. Once it had, he focused on the table and saw that it was empty. Of course, Joanna had never been there, but he wished now that he had dreamed about Hickok again, and not her.

His lips and mouth were parched. He needed water or, failing that, anything wet. He looked down and saw the whiskey bottle at his feet. It was the one he had used to wash his wound. He picked it up and looked at it. There was about an inch of liquor left at the bottom of the bottle. Whiskey was not the ideal thing to drink on an empty stomach. He took a mouthful, swished it about, and then spat it on the floor. It would have to do. He put the bottle under the bar for safekeeping.

He wondered how long he had been here. It was still light out, but that didn't mean that he hadn't slept

through the night at least one of those times that he
had fallen unconscious. He couldn't see the sky to tell
time by, but he couldn't very well stick his head out
the door without having his head blown off.

There had to be a way out of here other than the front.
He thought briefly about throwing himself through one
of the windows, but he doubted that he'd be able to
move fast enough to avoid being shot. He was going
to have to look the place over again, but this time with
a totally different eye.

The first time he had been looking for a conventional
exit. This time he had to look for something else, some
way out of the building that was never meant to be a
way out.

He assumed, since the building was locked up tight
to keep him in, that he had the run of the place. Now
that his head was somewhat clearer, he understood that
as long as he was inside, he'd have freedom to move
around. He had to put that freedom to good use.

He went back down the hallway to the back door and
tried it again. If anything, it felt shut even tighter than
before. He went back up the hallway slowly, examining
the walls. On his right the wall bordered the saloon. On
his left was the outside wall. He took out his gun and
tapped the wall with the butt. It was solid wood. The
place had been built a long time ago, when they were
building them well.

He went back into the saloon and walked in a circle, along the walls, tapping them. The only wall he
didn't check was the front one. He didn't think he'd
be allowed near the windows without drawing fire.

When he finished with the walls he walked around
again, first the hall and then the main room, testing
the floor with his boot heels. It all seemed to be solid

underneath, most likely hard-packed dirt. Even if he had something to pry the board up with, he'd need something to dig with—and the strength with which to do the digging.

Whoever was out there seemed to have fashioned an airtight prison.

TEN

Duke.

Clint wondered once again what had become of Duke. Where had the big gelding gotten to? Was he running free somewhere in town, or had the assailant gotten ahold of him and tied him down someplace?

If Duke was free, then maybe he was Clint's way out of his prison. If Duke was true to form—and free—he'd be somewhere around the saloon. If he was not on the street in front, then he'd be in the back. He would know where Clint Adams was, and would not stray far.

Duke, however, was not a trained "pet." He had never been trained, for instance, to respond to a whistle from Clint. Somehow, Clint was going to have to ascertain exactly where the big gelding was.

Before that, though, Clint had to finish his survey of his prison. He had not yet thoroughly checked the area behind the bar.

There were shelves on the wall behind the bar, but beneath the shelves was plain wall. Clint checked the wall to see if there were any loose boards, but he found none. He then checked the floorboards, but they were tight as well. Just for his own satisfaction he sat on the floor, braced his back against the bar, and kicked out at the wall. He hoped to splinter a board or two, but they held fast. All he managed to do was give himself a pounding headache. He sat there for a few moments, hoping that the pounding would subside.

It took longer than that, but finally he felt able to stand. He looked up at the ceiling, wondering if there was a way out there. Maybe a trapdoor to the roof. He studied the ceiling intently, but could not find a telltale outline that might indicate a trapdoor. There were some bullet holes, but little else. No escape there.

Clint was starting to realize what men in prison felt like, and they usually had a lot less room to roam around in than he had.

Clint came around the bar and went back into the hallway. He wondered what would happen if he just stayed in that hallway and didn't come out again. Would his assailant think that he had somehow escaped, and come across the street for a look? Or was he so confident that his saloon was inescapable that he would be patient and stay where he was?

Clint figured his assailant was probably perfectly prepared to exhibit as much patience as needed. The person would not have set this whole thing up if he was the impatient type. Also, that kind of patience had to be tempered with intelligence. That simply meant that whoever had lured him here and thrust him into this situation was smart enough to set it up, and patient enough to execute it according to plan. Many of the men Clint had thought of so far would not have those two qualities.

He walked down the hall to the sealed back door again. He kept returning to it as his way out. He leaned into it with all his strength, but it did not budge. He tried to peer through the cracks on either side of the door, but he could not. There was not even any light filtering through, that's how completely sealed the door was. Clint was about to give up on the door when he suddenly realized that maybe there was one place in which the door was not so completely sealed. He dropped down onto the floor and peered underneath. Sure enough, there was some light, and he was even able to see outside.

The only problem was, there was nothing to see.

Across the street the shooter had been watching Clint Adams as Adams inspected his prison. By now he hoped that Adams had finally found the only other exit from the saloon. If Adams didn't get out of the saloon at all, that would make all of the shooter's other preparations go to waste. If Clint Adams, the famous Gunsmith, gave up and died in that saloon, the shooter was going to be very disappointed.

ELEVEN

Clint couldn't see anything underneath the door, but after a few moments he thought he heard something. Horses rarely stood completely still and quiet. He was picking up the sounds of shifting hooves and an occasional exhalation.

Could it be Duke? Had he sensed that Clint was inside the saloon? Was he now simply waiting outside, in the back, for him?

"Duke?" Clint called. "Duke, boy?"

He hoped he was calling loud enough for the horse to hear, but not loud enough for his assailant to hear across the street.

"Duke? Is that you? Come on, big fella. Come over to the door."

Even if the horse didn't understand exactly what he was saying, he would certainly recognize his voice. He kept calling, even though at one point he began to wonder if this was a dream, too. Maybe he was still sitting on the floor behind the bar, unconscious.

"Duke, come on, boy!"

Across the street the shooter was gathering up his belongings. His rifles, his pistols, the food and water he had brought along for himself, and his blanket. It was time to move to his next location. He felt fairly confident that within the next half hour or so, Clint Adams would have freed himself from the saloon. If he did that, then everything would be right on schedule.

Finally Clint saw a horse's hooves through the crack beneath the door. He couldn't have sworn they were Duke's, but he hoped they were.

"Duke? Come on, big fella. Over to the door. That's it, I'm over here. . . ."

He just kept talking until the horse moved right up to the door.

"That's it," Clint said, "I'm here. I can't get out. Come on, Duke, kick it in. Come on!"

From the position of the hinges Clint knew that the door opened inward. He hoped that would make it easier for Duke to open it by kicking it.

There was a thud as Duke's—and by now he was sure it *was* Duke's—nose banged into the door. Following that the horse seemed to be testing the door with a front hoof, scraping at it. Clint could see that door gave slightly when Duke's hoof hit it.

He got up off the floor and moved to one side as he continued to implore the horse to kick the door in. He could picture the big black gelding as Duke turned around and then lifted both hind legs, kicking out at the door. It took but one well-placed kick and the door not only opened with a loud, splintering sound but also flew off its hinges. If Clint had been standing in the way he'd certainly have been knocked unconscious, if not killed. However, he wasn't standing in the way, and as a result he was not only alive . . . he was also free!

• • •

The shooter heard the splintering sound as he was setting up his new location. He smiled, spread his blanket, and then went to the window and began laying out his weapons.

It wouldn't be long now.

TWELVE

Clint had several options, and he paused to consider them right there in the shattered saloon doorway. First, he could mount up and ride Duke right out of the town of Patience and never look back. If he did that, however, he would never know who had lured him there.

Second, he could mount Duke and ride out and watch from a distance until his assailant also left town. If he did, that there was always a chance that the assailant (he preferred to think of the assailant as a man, at this point) might slip away, unseen. That would leave him free to try again at some future time. On the surface that might not have seemed so bad. It would give Clint time to heal.

The third option was one that Clint preferred, however. He would stay in town and try to find the assailant. He wanted very badly to know who had set this trap, and why. He still wasn't sure how long he had been here, but he preferred to think that no more than two days had passed. He was at least two days hungry.

"How about you, big boy?" he asked, rubbing Duke's nose. "You hungry, too?"

Duke pressed his nose into Clint's hand and shifted his hooves. How long had the big gelding been waiting back here? Had he escaped the notice of the assailant,

or had the assailant simply ignored the horse in favor
of the man?

Clint soon found the answer. He dipped his hand into
his saddlebag, intending to get out some beef jerky to
eat, but there was none. He *knew* that he had some in
there, and that he had not eaten it along the way. Of
course, he could have been mistaken, so he searched
through both saddlebags to see if anything else was
missing. His coffeepot was still there, as well as his eating utensils, but anything that might have been edible
was gone. The assailant had obviously gotten close
enough to Duke to go through the saddlebags. What
other mischief had the assailant wrought?

Clint pulled out a rolled-up shirt and carefully
unrolled it. Inside was secreted his little Colt New
Line belly gun. The man had either missed it, or . . .
he checked the gun's action and found it in working
order. He checked the loads, and they were fine. He
tucked the gun away in his belt. Obviously the assailant
had missed it . . . but what about the rifle?

Clint removed his rifle from the scabbard and
inspected it. It didn't take him long to catch the damage. The firing pin had been filed down. If he had not
checked the weapon, it would have failed him at some
critical moment. He slid the rifle back into place.

Now he checked Duke over carefully, to be sure that
the big gelding had not been damaged in some way.
The animal seemed sound, but the assailant, on one
occasion at least, had been able to approach the horse
without incident . . . or had he?

His new position fully prepared, the shooter unwound
his neckerchief from the bite on his hand to inspect it.
If he hadn't been quick, the Gunsmith's black horse

might have taken off his entire hand. The bite wound, on the edge of his left hand, seemed clean enough. He had washed it out immediately with whiskey, and it did not seem to be showing any sign of infection.

He probably should have shot the damned horse on sight, but he didn't come here to kill an animal, he came to kill a man. If he saw the horse again, though, he did not rule out shooting it this time. He would certainly do that before he'd allow the animal to sink his teeth into him again.

Clint decided to set Duke free. The horse had rescued him, but how long would it take the assailant to realize that killing Duke, or injuring him, would devastate Clint? Neither did Clint want the horse's safety to become an issue if and when he managed to find his assailant. He had to make sure that the horse was out of harm's way.

He removed his saddle from Duke's broad, powerful back and set it down against the rear wall of the saloon.

"Okay, big fella," Clint said, "get going."

Duke didn't move.

"Come on, I want you out of town so I don't have to worry about you. Go."

Still the big gelding did not move. He stood there, staring at Clint.

"Look," Clint said, "I know you think I'm helpless without you, but get moving. I'll be fine." When the big horse still did not move, Clint moved behind him and slapped him on the rump . . . hard!

"Go!"

This time Duke moved. He trotted away a few yards, then stopped and looked back.

Clint waved his arms and said, "Go. Wait outside of town."

Duke shook his head as if in protest, then turned and galloped off. Clint waited until the horse was out of sight, then went over and sat down on his saddle to figure out his next move.

Actually, the next move was obvious. He had to try to find the person behind this whole thing. That meant working his way around behind the buildings across the street. He wanted to find out the who and the why, but more important than that was getting the upper hand. If it came down to kill or be killed, then he'd have to forget about the who and the why and make sure that he was the one who came out alive.

From his vantage point the shooter could see the big black horse leaving town. That was a good move by Clint Adams. Now the animal's safety could not be used against him. Also, it was proof enough that Adams *had* managed to escape from the saloon, just as he'd been expected to.

The horse had been unsaddled, which meant that Adams had also gone through his saddlebags. By now he knew that the shooter had removed all his food. The shooter wondered if Adams had examined his rifle closely enough to know that it was useless.

He settled down to watch the street. Adams would surely want to work his way across the street to where the shooter previously was. He lifted one of his rifles and held it in his hands. He was pleased that Adams had not chosen to ride out of town and escape. If he had, then a new plan would have had to be put into effect, and it would have taken much longer.

He was glad that the whole plan would be played out right here in Patience.

THIRTEEN

Clint worked his way as far away from the saloon as he could while staying behind the buildings on his side of the street. When he could go no farther, he found an alley and walked through to the main street. Cautiously, he stepped out from the alley and trotted across the street to the other side.

Once he was there, he found a doorway and settled into it for a few moments. He surveyed the other side of the street and couldn't see anything. He wondered if the shooter was still in place across from the saloon. There was only one way to find out.

He left the doorway and worked his way up the street, away from the saloon. At the first alley he came to he turned in and walked all the way to the back. There was a high wooden fence there, and he had to climb over it, which didn't do his head any good. When he dropped down on the other side he squatted down and waited for the pounding in his head to stop. When it did, he stood up and started along the backs of the buildings. He was going to have to guess when he was behind the building across from the saloon, and then look for a way to get inside without alerting his attacker.

As he approached what he thought was the building he wanted, he slowed down. There was a window in the back wall, and as he looked inside he saw that it was a storeroom. There was a curtained doorway that he could not see beyond. Slowly, he moved to the rear door and put his left hand on the doorknob. With his right hand he drew his gun. The doorknob turned, and right then he knew what he would find inside.

Nothing.

From his vantage point the shooter could see Clint Adams enter the room where he had been set up the previous two days. Once again, Clint had not disappointed him. He had found the right building on the first try.

The shooter sighted down the barrel of one of his rifles and waited for Clint Adams to move into position. The other rifles were close at hand, loaded and ready to be fired.

Clint pushed aside the curtain in the doorway and entered the front room. There were enough indications that someone had been there for Clint to know that he had the right place. There were spent shells littering the floor, some empty food cans, and many crushed-out cigarettes. He moved to the front window, which had no glass left, and peered out. He could see right into the saloon across the street. This was certainly the point from where his assailant had herded him into the saloon and then kept him pinned down.

The question now was, where had he gone?

Still sighting down the barrel, the shooter watched as Clint Adams stood in the window and stared across the street. Framed in the window like that, he was an easy target.

Slowly, he squeezed the trigger. . . .

• • •

Clint heard the shot and reacted immediately. He threw himself aside and to the floor as the bullet struck the wall next to the window. He crawled along the wall as lead began to fly through the window.

He was pinned down again.

Lead chewed up the wood of the floor and the walls, sending splinters flying around the room. Clint guessed that this time his assailant was in a room higher up, on a second floor, or possibly even on a rooftop. He stayed on the floor, pressed right to the wall, and waited for the barrage of lead and wood splinters to end. When it finally did, the quiet was deafening. He sat up straighter, but stayed on the floor. He wished he had his hat to raise above the level of the window. He figured if he showed his face the shooting would start again.

Still, he had been a perfect target, framed in the window as he had been, and the assailant had missed him—probably deliberately. Clint thought that the man—or woman—was sending him a message, and he thought he knew what the message was.

The town was *his* battleground, and the rules were his as well. He was telling Clint that no matter where he was, he could be had.

Well, Clint has gotten the message, all right, but it was time for him to send one of his own as well.

Of course, that was a hell of a lot easier said than done, wasn't it?

Still with his back to the wall, Clint looked around the room carefully. He was starting to think that this cat-and-mouse game could go on for days. If he was going to last, he was going to have to get some food.

There was none to be had here, though. The assailant must have had some here for himself, but he'd made sure that he had removed every crumb or other remnant of it.

He moved his legs, trying to keep them from stiffening. He was going to have to make a move for the back room, and get out of the building the way he had gotten in. He reached up and removed the makeshift bandage he had fashioned for his wound from his head. The flash of white would make him too good a target, if and when the assailant decided to end the game.

He looked around for something to throw. There was a piece of shelving nearby, about three feet long. That would do. He reached for it and dragged it over. Taking hold of it, he got into a crouch, then tossed the shelving out the window. At the same time he sprang to his feet and ran for the curtained doorway. Halfway there he realized that there was no shooting, and he stopped. He turned and walked back to the window, looking outside. Still no shooting. He decided to press it and climbed out the window onto the boardwalk. Still no shots.

Had the sonofabitch moved again?

The shooter stared down at Clint Adams and smiled. He could see the puzzlement on Adams's face, and probably some annoyance. There was no fear there, though. Not yet, and he wouldn't kill him until there was.

He gathered up his arms and moved on to his next position.

FOURTEEN

Clint stepped out into the middle of the street and stood there with his hands on his hips. Was this another message? Was the assailant now giving him the run of the town? Daring him to find him?

This was possibly the most helpless Clint had ever felt, and he found it oddly intriguing.

He crossed over to the saloon and entered it again. It had been his prison for what . . . two days? Now he was back there, but he didn't think there was much danger of being trapped there again. They were beyond that stage.

He looked around for his hat, then realized that he had not had it with him when he was "herded" into the saloon. He went back outside and looked around until he found it behind the horse trough. He slapped it against his thigh a few times, raising dust, then put it on his head gingerly.

Since he seemed to have the run of the town, he decided to look at it. He might as well take the opportunity that was being given him to acquaint himself with the battlefield.

Rather than pick one side of the street over the other, he decided to walk right down the center of the main street. Maybe by doing that he'd send a message of his own to his opponent. Clint Adams may be weak from hunger and a head wound, but he wasn't scared.

Not yet, anyway.

It didn't take Clint long to ascertain that the battlefield was a small one, as towns went. The town was only about three blocks long and had virtually no side streets, except for some alleys that were not wide enough to be called streets.

At the end of the three blocks was a livery stable. It was doubtful that he would find anything inside, but he decided to look, anyway. The front doors were unlocked, and he swung one open all the way, so he'd have some light inside.

All of the stalls appeared to be empty. From the way the place smelled, it had been a while since any horses had been kept there. He looked down at the ground and saw some hoofprints. A horse *had* been in here recently, but it had not been put up there. These were probably the tracks of his assailant's horse. He started to crouch down to examine them more closely when he heard something behind him. He turned in time to see the door swinging shut. He moved, but not quickly enough to stop the door from closing. By the time he reached it, it was not only closed, but also locked. He was in the dark, and locked in.

"Adams."

He barely heard the voice. It was so faint that he thought he must have imagined it.

"Adams."

It was a rasp, a whisper, and he had to press his ear to the door to hear it.

"Look in the last stall on the right, Adams," the whispery voice said. "Take a look."

Then there was laughter, retreating laughter as the assailant walked away from the stable. Clint turned his back to the door, but did not move until his eyes had adjusted to the darkness.

He thought about the voice, but it had been too low, too hoarse for him to identify it. No matter how he tried to magnify it in his mind, he couldn't.

When his eyes had adjusted to the darkness, he began to move forward. There had to be a storm lamp around somewhere. For some reason he did not think that he was meant to be left in the dark. He reached into his pocket to see if he had any lucifer matches. He took three out and put two back. He didn't want to waste one by lighting it and using it to find the lamp. If he was right, then the lamp would have to be where he could . . . there it was. He bumped into it with one flailing hand, then grabbed it before it could fall from its perch. He set fire to the match and lit the lamp. He adjusted the flame so the inside of the livery was bathed in a not-too-bright yellow glow. The lamp didn't feel like it had that much oil, and he didn't want it to burn too fast.

Now that he had enough light, he want back to look at the tracks on the dirt floor of the livery. The tracks were of a shod horse, but there was no way he could tell them from any other tracks. There was not anything remarkable or memorable about them.

He stood up and thought about the voice again. He was so intent on trying to identify it that he had not even concentrated on *what* was being said. Now he recalled that the voice had told him to look in the last stall on the right. He wondered what he would find there. A message from his hunter?

He approached the stalls now with a feeling of excitement. Maybe there would be something there that would shed some light on this whole affair. Mixed with the excitement, however, was some apprehension.

As he passed the other stalls along the way he held the lamp up and checked them as well. They were all empty. He approached that final stall and held the lamp ahead of him. He stopped next to the stall, staring straight ahead. Finally he turned his head and looked inside.

The first thing he noticed was the red blood on the yellow hay. The stall had been filled with hay, and lying on it, as if thrown there, was a body. The body was that of a woman, and although he couldn't see her face, he could see her long, blond hair. How many women had he known who had blond hair? How many blond women was he close to?

He had known many, but the one who came to mind was Sandy Spillane.

"Jesus," he said, and moved into the stall.

He set the lamp down, away from the hay so he wouldn't start a fire, and reached for the body. As he turned her over, he steeled himself to see the face of Sandy Spillane.

The body flopped onto its back, and her blond hair was matted to her face by blood. Gently he plucked the hair away so he could get a clear look at her face.

He had never seen the woman before in his life.

FIFTEEN

He stared at the dead woman for a few moments. He realized that she was Sandy Spillane's size and shape and, in life, might have almost been her twin. When he recovered from the shock of finding her he leaned over her to examine her more closely. Her hair had not been matted to her forehead by accident. There was blood on her head, and it had been put there deliberately. It was slightly smeared, but he thought he could make it out. It looked like the initials "SS."

Her throat had been cut, and then whoever had done it had dipped their fingers in the blood and written the initials "SS" on her forehead.

Was it a coincidence that those were Sandy Spillane's initials? Not when you took into account that the dead woman was almost a double for the lady bounty hunter. No, this was another message, but what did it mean? Did it mean that at another time, in another place, Sandy Spillane had been killed? Or that she would be killed after him?

And who was this poor woman? Just someone who had crossed the killer's path at the wrong time? He forced himself to go through her pockets, but he didn't find anything that would identify her.

He picked up the lamp and backed out of the stall, taking one last look at the woman. He walked back to the front of the stable and sat down on a bale of hay.

Was this the killer's way of telling him that the reason for all of this had to do with something he and Sandy had been involved in? Could it be that Fast Draw League thing, after all? Could it be Jason Sharp behind this, after all?

He stood up and took the lamp to the front doors with him. He tried them. They were still locked. The oil in the lamp was almost gone. He might have had enough left to make a quick circuit of the stable, to try to find another way out.

He found a side door, but it was sealed on the other side, and he didn't have Duke to kick it in. He moved quickly, testing boards and the hard-packed floor. Once again he was struck by how well built this stable was for a ghost town, as the saloon had been.

Suddenly the flame in the lamp flickered and went out. He put it down on the ground and stood still until his eyes had adjusted to the dark again. Now he was locked in the dark with a dead body. How long, he wondered, was he going to be kept locked in this time?

SIXTEEN

For want of something better to do, Clint returned to the back stall, lit a match, and looked at the woman again. He still didn't know her, but there was no doubt in his mind that she was supposed to symbolize Sandy Spillane. The bloody initials on her head made that very plain.

What was also very plain now was that he was dealing with a killer, pure and simple, someone to whom taking a life meant nothing. He had killed this woman just to make a point.

Was he just trying to make some kind of point? Did this mean that he was going after Sandy next? Or was the killer just trying to play games with Clint's mind?

The match burned down, and Clint made sure he didn't drop it into the hay. Once again he was shrouded in total darkness, left alone with the dead woman and his own thoughts—and right now his thoughts were about the dead woman. How had she come to be here? Had she been killed elsewhere and brought here? Clint frowned. That would mean she had been dead for days, and she didn't look as if she'd been dead for days, she looked like she was fresher than that. That meant that he had brought her here alive and had killed her here. And *that* meant that he had to have kept her locked up somewhere.

And if that was the case, how many others did he have locked up? Why stop with a Sandy Spillane look-alike? Why not move on to a Katy Littlefeather double, and then a double of Anne Archer?

Now that he thought of it, it made sense. Keep teasing him by letting him find bodies that resemble friends of his. Why stop at women? Why not let him find a Rick Hartman double, or a Bat Masterson stand-in?

Obviously, whoever the killer was he had studied his prey for a long time before putting this plan into effect. The telegram had just the right tone to it, and the dead woman was almost the spitting image of Sandy.

What was next?

And when?

If there were other people being kept prisoner in this town, people waiting to be killed, he had to find them, but before he could do that, he had to get out of here.

He had one match left. If he used it to try to find a shovel, or a pitchfork, he had better find one on the first try. With some sort of hand tool he might be able to pry one of the doors open.

What he needed was something that would burn. He needed to build himself a fire someplace where it wouldn't burn the whole barn down.

In the dark he found a spot on the hard-packed dirt floor and piled some hay up. He took the hay from the stall where the dead woman was. When he had enough of it he lit the match and used it to look around for a shovel, or something. When he didn't find one right away and the match was dying down, he dropped it onto the pile of hay.

While the hay flared, giving him some light to work by, he went over to one of the stalls and kicked at it until some of the wood splintered. He picked up the pieces and dropped them onto the fire. The wood would burn longer than the hay. He didn't know how long the killer meant to keep him in there, and he might as well have some light while he was waiting.

He was sure that at one point the killer would come back and let him out. Nothing would be accomplished by keeping him there. He'd either be let out, or else there was another way out and he was going to have to find it. That was better than just sitting on his hands.

He looked around for something that would burn, but found nothing. He hated to do it, but he went back to the body and tore shreds from her shirt. He was careful not to expose her while doing it, pulling the shirt out of her pants and taking strips from the shirttail.

Using the strips, he tied some hay tightly together so it would burn for a while, and then tied it to the end of a large piece of wood he kicked loose from a stall.

With his makeshift torch he went up to the hayloft to see if there was any way out from there. What he found up there surprised him, although it probably shouldn't have.

It was a second body.

He held the torch high, staring at it a while before approaching it. From behind it looked like a dark-haired woman. When he turned her over he saw that she was an Indian . . . and almost the spitting image of Katy Littlefeather.

"Jesus," he said, passing one hand over his face.

Examining her, he found that rather than having her throat cut like the Sandy Spillane double, she had been strangled.

He stood up and continued to inspect the loft, hoping that he would not find an Anne Archer look-alike in the process.

• • •

The killer smiled.

By now Clint Adams must have found the second body. By now the Gunsmith knew that the killer meant business.

Maybe by now the goddamned Gunsmith knew that he was in a world of trouble.

SEVENTEEN

After a complete inspection of the hayloft there was good news and bad news. The good news was that there were no more bodies up there. The bad news was that there was no way out through the hayloft.

His torch was petering out, so he climbed back down to where his fire was still going nicely. He stomped out the remains of the torch and then by the light of the fire began looking the interior of the stable over again, for a way out. There had to be one. He was convinced that, as with the saloon, the killer knew that he would find a way out. If he didn't, the killer would probably be very disappointed in him.

Damn, but he hated being in this situation! If the killer had walked into the stable right at that moment, unarmed, Clint would have taken great enjoyment out of shooting him dead. The man must be stark, raving mad. He'd *have* to be to kill two innocent women with no regard for their lives. They probably had no idea why they were dying. A man who would do something like that had no right to live, and when Clint found him, he was going to take care of that little thing.

First, of course, he had to get out of the stable.

He approached one wall of the stable and kicked at it viciously. Unlike the wood of the stalls, it did not splinter. What he needed was something to hammer it out with, or something to weaken it. What weakened wood?

The answer was obvious.

Fire!

He turned and looked at his camp fire. Did he dare set fire to one wall? If he did, it was possible that the entire stable would go up in flames and, after that, the town.

Jesus, what the hell was the difference? It was a ghost town, and if the killer had a fire to deal with, maybe he'd get careless. Besides, the barn was off separate from the town, so it would probably burn to the ground with no further damage. It would also give the two dead women a resting place.

Of course, it might do the same for him, but that was a chance he was going to have to take.

He picked up a burning piece of wood, grabbed a handful of hay, and carried them to one of the walls. He chose one that faced away from the town. He set the hay down at the base of the wall, then touched the burning wood to it. It flared and burned, and he dropped the piece of wood onto it and backed away. He was surprised at how quickly the flames crawled up the wall. He'd never seen anything move so fast. It was as if the fire were hungry and the wall was its food. He had hoped that the small portion of the wall would burn through before the entire wall caught, but he had underestimated the compatibility of the fire and the dry wood.

Suddenly the entire wall was burning, and the heat was becoming oppressive. Also, the wall was giving off billowing smoke, which would soon fill the interior of the stable.

In his effort to escape, he just might have sealed his own death warrant.

• • •

The killer saw the smoke. The fool had somehow set the stable on fire. If he didn't get him out, he'd die in the fire, and the killer didn't want that. That would rob him of his right to kill Clint Adams.

Quickly the killer left his position, ran from the building, and hurried toward the stable.

Clint knew he'd made a mistake, but it had been a calculated risk.

Maybe he should have calculated on it a little more.

Clint had hoped to be able to break through a portion of the burning wall, but the heat was so intense that he probably would have burned to a crisp trying to do it. Then again, if he didn't try it he'd probably burn to death anyway, if he didn't suffocate first. Already he couldn't breathe, and his eyes were streaming tears.

He was about to try it when something unexpected happened.

The front doors opened.

He stood where he was, staring at the open doors. The smoke, long looking for a way to escape from the inside of the barn, began to funnel out, and he suspected that his best move would be to follow it out.

He drew his gun and, under cover of the smoke, ran toward the doors.

As he reached the outside he did not pause to enjoy the air that struck his face and entered his lungs. Instead he threw himself to the ground, rolled and rolled, and came to a stop in a crouch, trying to see everywhere at one time. He needn't have taken the precaution.

There was no one around.

Apparently the killer had seen the smoke and, worried that Clint would die before *he* could kill him, had rushed to the rescue, then hurried away.

Clint stood, holstered his gun, and now took a moment to cleanse his lungs. He looked at the stable, which by now had become totally engulfed by the flames. The stable was far enough from the next building, however, that barring a heavy wind, the town should be safe from the flames.

Clint looked around and saw a horse trough nearby. He walked over to it and washed his hands, neck, and face. He then pumped some fresh water into his hands and drank it. He took an extra moment to tear a piece of his shirt, soak it and use it to clean his eyes. He knew he was a sitting duck, but he also knew that the killer wasn't ready to kill him yet.

He wasn't through taunting him yet.

At that moment Clint realized that he had a clear-cut advantage over the killer.

The man wasn't ready to kill him yet.

He, on the other hand, wanted nothing more than to kill the madman on sight.

From a position of hiding, the killer watched with relief as Clint Adams came rolling out of the stable. He watched as Adams bent over the horse trough, his back an inviting target. In fact, the killer even drew his gun and sighted down the barrel at his quarry's back, but he quickly lowered the gun. That would be too easy. When Clint Adams finally died, it was not going to be as easy, or as quick, as a bullet in the back.

Satisfied that Clint Adams was in condition to continue the game, the killer turned and started back to his new position.

EIGHTEEN

Clint tried to put himself into the mind of the killer. Except for that first assault, which had taken place from a ground-floor location, the killer would have to be high up to keep tabs on him.

Roof or second floor?

Probably a second-floor window. He'd want his back covered, and that would not be the case out in the open on a rooftop.

No matter where Clint went in town, he couldn't be sure whether he'd be in sight of the killer. Knowing that, he decided not to worry about it. He needed someplace to think, someplace where *his* back would be covered by walls. There was only one place in town he could think of going to.

He started walking back up the street, but this time he picked a side. He mounted the boardwalk on the side away from the saloon. He had spotted the location he wanted on his way to the livery, and it was on this side of the street. Before long he reached his destination and entered without looking back.

He closed the door behind him and surveyed the room. It looked like any other sheriff's office he had ever been in, except that the gunrack on the wall was empty, and everything was covered with a layer of dust.

The desk was intact, as was the chair behind it, and he walked over and sat down, not paying the dust any mind. His clothes were so dirty from the saloon, and from the fire—not to mention rolling around in the street—that a little dust was the least of his problems.

In fact, a *lot* of dust was the least of his problems.

The killer watched as Clint Adams entered the sheriff's office. He smiled, and was thankful for those psychology courses he had taken in that college back East.

Clint stared at the desk and then, for want of something to do, began opening the drawers.

First the three on the right.

Empty.

Then the three on the left.

All empty.

Then he opened the middle drawer. It was not empty. There was an envelope in it. A white envelope, and written on the front was his name.

"Sonofabitch!" he shouted, and slammed the drawer shut so hard that the wood splintered, and the drawer came loose from the desk. It fell to the floor, striking his knees first.

He stood up, as if the drawer had scalded him, and stared down at it.

How?

How had the killer known that he would come here?

For the first time since arriving in town, since this ordeal had started, he was close to feeling fear.

The killer was very satisfied with himself.

By now, he thought, even though he was dealing with the Gunsmith, the fear should be starting to set in.

• • •

"Calm yourself, damn it!" Clint told himself. "The bastard could have left an envelope somewhere in every building in town, just so you'd react like this."

He bent over and retrieved the envelope from where it had fallen on the floor. It wasn't sealed. He slipped the flap out and found a small piece of paper folded inside. He took it out and set the envelope down on the top of the desk. He unfolded the piece of paper. It was a note.

It said: LOOK IN THE CELLS.

Clint crumpled the paper in his hand and squeezed it tightly. He didn't even have to look to know what he would find. For a moment he almost decided *not* to go and look, but he finally decided that he had to.

Still holding the note tightly in his hand, he walked into the back, where the cells were. There were three of them.

Jesus Christ, he thought, please don't let there be a body in each of them.

Slowly, filled with apprehension, he approached the first cell.

Empty.

He didn't breathe a sigh of relief. He didn't dare. He moved onto the second cell.

Empty.

Now for the third, and he was sure to find something there.

It was on the bunk, lying on its side with its back to him. It was as if the man were sleeping.

He was mildly surprised to find that it was a man's body. He had been expecting it to be a woman's.

The body was well dressed, wearing a dark suit and well-polished shoes. He could see the high polish on the shoes even from where he stood. Sitting on the pillow, just above the dark-haired head, was a bowler hat.

It took him only a moment to realize that the body represented one of his best friends.

Bat Masterson.

NINETEEN

Clint was momentarily confused.

He had been assuming, since the first two bodies represented Sandy Spillane and Katy Littlefeather, that this whole thing had something to do with them, and with Anne Archer—or with something that the four of them had been involved in. Now, however, with Bat Masterson thrown in, it looked as if the killer was only trying to show Clint that he knew who the people closest to him were.

Clint approached the man and turned his head so he could see the face. The damned body was still warm. The man had been killed only hours ago, probably while Clint had been in the livery stable. He didn't know the man, but that didn't stop him from lamenting his death.

"Sorry, friend," Clint said, "but you just got caught up in something that didn't even concern you."

Clint went through the man's pockets, but he didn't expect to find anything, and he did not. He left the man there and went back into the office.

Once again he wondered how the killer had known that he would head for the sheriff's office. And how he had been so sure that he planted the body there, and the note.

It was becoming very evident that Clint was not deal-

ing with a simple mind, nor a normal one. In his mad-
ness, the killer was probably very cunning and extremely intelligent. When Clint thought about it calmly—or
as calmly as he could after all he had been through—it
made sense for the killer to assume that he would come
here, to the office of the law. After all, Clint had been
a lawman for many years. In fact, maybe this was the
killer's way of telling him that he knew that, too.

Clint walked to the window, which had dusty curtains on it, and peered out. He studied the second-floor
windows of the buildings across the street, but could
see nothing. That didn't mean that the man wasn't up
there, though, looking down at him.

It was dusk outside, and Clint decided that he would
spend the night here. If the killer wanted him tonight,
he was going to have to come and get him.

Before he could settle in, though, he had to make
sure he was secure. He went into the back again, past
the cells, and found the back door. He tried it, and found
that he needn't have worried about it. It was sealed shut
on the outside. That was fine with him. He couldn't get
out, but the killer couldn't get in, either.

Next he tried the bars on the windows in the cells.
He had to reach over the dead man to do it, but he was
sure now that the bars were secure. No one was going
to get in that way.

He went back into the office and closed the con-
necting door. There was an old coffeepot on top of a
potbellied stove. He took the pot and set it down right
in front of the door. If someone tried to open the door,
the pot would fall over, or scrape the floor. Either way,
it would wake him.

He sat in the chair behind the desk and put his heels

up on the desk. If he couldn't get any food, he was going to have to get some rest. His eyes felt gritty, partially from the smoke and partially from fatigue.

He closed his eyes, not at all sure that he could sleep, and in seconds, he was.

He dreamed about Anne Archer.

Anne had the most incredible eyebrows. They were heavy, so much so that they appeared to be darker than her red hair. Her mouth, too, was amazing. Full, inviting, the upper lip almost as full as the lower. Her face was the most arresting thing about her, but that did not mean that she did not have a beautiful body. She did. In fact, in his dream, he was in bed with her. She was sitting astride him, riding him with his penis buried deep inside her. He pulled her down to him, kissed her breasts, biting the hard nipples, running his hands over her back and then down to her firm buttocks. She moaned when he squeezed her there, sucking hard on one of her nipples. He felt himself swelling inside her, very near to bursting, and she felt it, too.

She sat up on him again and smiled down at him.

"My God," she said, "you feel as if you might blow my head off when you explode. . . ."

"Anne . . ." he said, but suddenly she put her head back, way back so that he could see her lovely neck stretching taut, and then suddenly something was wrong . . . something was happening . . . there was blood on her neck, a line of blood that was becoming wider, as if someone had cut her throat . . . and then it *was* a wound, a yawning wound growing wider and wider as her head went back farther and farther. . . . Blood flowed down over her chest and belly, onto him, warm, wet, and sticky, and then he knew that if he couldn't catch it in time her head was going to fall. . . . Jesus, it was going to fall. . . .

He sat bolt upright in the chair, drenched in cold sweat and, obscenely, he had an erection, a huge, throbbing erection, and he was afraid to move for fear that it would explode. . . .

TWENTY

After a few moments he was able to rise shakily to his feet. The dream had been so vivid that he had to look down at himself to make sure he wasn't covered with Anne Archer's blood. He had no water handy, so he just wiped his sweaty face with his shirtsleeves. He peeked out the window without moving the curtain and saw that it was dark. He must have slept for at least several hours, maybe more. Christ, but he could have used a cup of coffee. How long had it been since he'd eaten? Long enough for the hunger pains to have become almost unnoticeable.

He went back to the desk, perched his butt on the edge, took his gun out, and checked the loads. Then he realized that he intended to go out into the dark. Maybe under cover of darkness he could accomplish something. He doubted that the killer would be careless, so if something was going to happen, Clint was going to have to force the issue.

He wondered how many more bodies were scattered around town for him to find. Did the killer still have any live captives left? Maybe an Anne Archer look-alike? Or a Rick Hartman double? If he was holding any more people, and Clint could free them, then they'd have a numbers advantage.

Since the back door was sealed, he was going to have

to go out the front. Jesus, he thought, the killer must have spent weeks in this ghost town, setting this up, nailing doors shut all over town, strategically picking out his spots. He'd heard of fighting someone on their home ground, but this was ridiculous.

He holstered his gun and rubbed his hands over his face, which felt dry and gritty, like his eyes. He walked to the front door, took a deep breath, opened it, and stepped outside quickly. There would be no telltale light from inside the office, but if the man was watching he was bound to see him. Still, Clint kept to the shadows as he moved up the street, toward the livery. He could smell smoke on the air, and if he listened closely enough he could hear the sound of crackling wood. He couldn't have been asleep all that long if the stable was still burning. Or had the town caught fire, after all?

He worked his way up the street far enough to determine that the stable was indeed still burning and that the fire had not spread to the town—not yet, anyway.

Once he reached the end of the street, he hurriedly crossed to the other side. If, as he suspected, the killer had stationed himself on a second floor across from the jailhouse, then he was now out of sight.

Or was he?

As darkness fell, the killer collected his gear and moved to his next location. He figured that Clint Adams might use the sheriff's office to get some sleep. By the time Clint woke up, the killer had stationed himself on a second floor on the same side as the jailhouse.

Just as Clint was wondering whether he was out of sight, the killer—his night vision perfect—was watching him and grinning. He wondered if he shouldn't go ahead and put a bullet into an arm or a leg of the Gunsmith, just to let him know that he was *never* out of sight.

No, not yet. Let him wander around some in the dark. After all, there were more surprises for him to find around town.

Nestled in the shadows of a doorway, Clint considered his next move. Logically, if the killer was positioned across from the jail, there were four or five buildings he could possibly be in. Back doors were likely nailed shut, which meant that Clint was going to have to go in through the front, and he was going to have to do it without alerting the killer. How much of a chance did he have to succeed there? So far the killer had been ahead of him every step of the way, even to the point of predicting his next move.

The only way to outsmart this man was to do something totally unpredictable. But what?

TWENTY-ONE

It was too quiet, almost unnaturally so. Clint had been in ghost towns before, but he had always been able to hear them—the ghosts, that is. Oh, not that he believed in *real* ghosts, but he would always imagine that he could hear some of the old residents of ghost towns like this one. At this time of night you could imagine that you were hearing sounds from the saloon—music, voices, laughter. Here, in this town, it was as if even those imagined ghosts didn't want to be here, didn't approve of what was going on.

Unpredictable . . .

The unpredictable thing to do would have been to leave town. Walk straight out there to wherever Duke was waiting, mount up, and ride away. What would the killer do then? Did he have a contingency plan for that eventuality? Would he chase Clint? Or just plan another encounter sometime in the future?

No, leaving was still not an option that Clint was willing to consider. This had to end here, in Patience. Too many people had died because of him—because of both of them—to leave it for another time.

Time to make a move . . .

The killer frowned. Just for a moment—a matter of seconds, actually—he had lost sight of Clint Adams, and then saw him. He was across the street, moving in the shadows.

In those few seconds, the killer felt fear, only he didn't see it that way. What he told himself he felt was respect for a man of Clint Adams's abilities. Naturally, if he had lost sight of Adams, he *should* feel concern. Clint Adams was, after all, the Gunsmith, and the killer had gone to great lengths to make sure he had a clear advantage over such a man. He did not delude himself that he would have been Clint Adams's equal, face to face. Not with a gun. Intellectually, however, he was more than Adams's equal. He had already proven that to the satisfaction of both of them.

But the killer would never admit to fear.

Never.

Clint began to move up the street, keeping close to the buildings, stopping every so often in a doorway. It was more than a little disconcerting not knowing whether he was being watched. At least when he was in the saloon he knew that the killer was out there, across the street, watching him. This way he just had to hope that he'd managed to slip from the sheriff's office unnoticed. Of course, the chances that he had done that were slim. The killer had already proven himself to be formidable, possibly more formidable than any enemy Clint Adams had faced in his life—and that was saying quite a bit. Most of the men he had faced before, however, were more deadly with their gun than with their brain.

This man was quite the opposite. . . .

Briefly, Clint allowed himself to consider for a moment that it might be a woman. Even the low, raspy voice he had heard in the livery could have been a woman's, but he chose to disregard the possibility once again. He couldn't accept that a woman could exhibit the degree of viciousness needed to kill the three people who had been killed so far.

Or maybe he just preferred to think that he had never done anything to a woman that would have brought her to this.

Somehow it would have been more frightening to think that a woman was doing this to him. Why? Didn't he think a woman was capable of outthinking him to this degree? When it came right down to it, if it were only a matter of intelligence, he *might* accept that it could be a woman. Factor in the killings, however, and he chose to believe that it was a man.

What about this, then? he asked himself. What if a woman thought the plan up and a man was executing it?

Now, *there* was a possibility.

He sat down in the doorway, a bit stunned by the thought but still finding himself unable to accept a woman's participation. A woman who wanted him dead would try to kill him, period. He still thought that the deaths of the other people made it more likely that the whole thing was a man's work.

What about the possibility that it was two men, then?

No, two men would find each wanting to take credit for it, and each would probably want the right to kill him. Besides, he didn't feel the presence of another man, and that's what it all came down to.

He felt *one* presence in town besides his own. He *sensed* it, and he had lived as long as he had by paying attention to the things he felt and sensed.

Back to basics, then. He was dealing with one man, and one mind, and there had to be a way to outwit him. Things had gone so well to this point that the man *had* to be feeling a certain degree of . . . *smug* satisfaction, or overconfidence.

Maybe Clint would be able to turn that back against him.

TWENTY-TWO

Wayne Gaines reigned in his horse as he topped a rise and looked down at the town of Patience, Oklahoma. Even from here it was plain that it was a dead town, a ghost town. Still, he had enough supplies left that he wasn't disappointed. Even if there was no one in the town, he would sleep tonight with a roof over his head, and that would be enough of a break from the past week to satisfy him. He had been on the trail for all of that time and was feeling particularly fatigued. All he wanted was a day or two of rest under a roof, and then he would be on his way again.

As he rode down toward Patience, he had no idea what was waiting ahead for him.

The killer was extremely satisfied with the way things were going. Even the fire in the barn had been nothing more than a momentary inconvenience. He was very satisfied with the way he had reacted to what had the potential to be a very disastrous situation. Adams could have died right there and then, and that was not the way the killer wanted things to go. No easy death for Clint Adams.

The killer was unaware that Fate was about to take a hand and that very shortly he would not be as satisfied as he was at that moment.

• • •

Clint ran his hand over his face and sat down in another doorway. The killer could have been in any of these buildings now, and suddenly he didn't have the strength to keep looking. He didn't know how long it had been since he'd eaten, or had water, but it was certainly having an effect on him, especially after his experience in the fire. He felt very close to total exhaustion. He needed food and water to help him recuperate, and he needed it badly.

Suddenly he thought he heard a horse approaching. For a moment he thought he might be imagining it, but then he saw the figure enter the street at the north end and begin to ride toward him.

A stranger? he wondered. Or an accomplice?

Whoever it was, he was sure to have food and water, and Clint suddenly saw a chance to survive.

For the moment the killer was unaware that a third presence had presented itself into his plan. He knew where Clint Adams was—in a doorway across from his location—and he was checking his weapons. He would regret his momentary lack of concentration.

Clint knelt down behind some old crates and drew his gun. He waited until the rider was abreast of him and then called out.

"Hold it right there."

The man stopped abruptly and raised his hands.

"What are you doing here?" Clint asked.

"Thought this was a ghost town."

"It is," Clint said. "I'll ask you again: What are you doing here?"

"Just lookin' for a place to rest for a while," the man

said. "I didn't know you were camped out here. I'll be on my way."

"You got any food and water?"

"Sure," the man said. "You need some? I'm willin' to share."

"I'm sorry to do this," Clint said, "but I'm in a situation where I can't trust anybody."

"I been in some situations like that myself," the man said.

"Drop your gun to the ground, and then toss your canteen over here."

"Sure," the man said. "Anything you say, friend."

He withdrew his gun from his holster easily with one hand and took his canteen from his saddle with the other.

At that moment that killer looked out the window and didn't like what he saw. Who the hell was the man on the horse? And what was he . . . He saw the man take his canteen from his saddle and knew what he was going to do with it.

He lifted his rifle to his shoulder, sighted down the barrel and fired.

Clint heard the shot and heard the impact of the bullet as it struck the man on the horse in the chest. The man had been in the act of tossing Clint his canteen, and Clint reached out with palsied hands to catch it. He even dropped his gun in his eagerness to grab the canteen, which seemed to be flying through the air in slow motion toward him.

As he closed his hands over the canteen, the man slid from his horse, hitting the ground with a thud, and his horse ran off down the street, taking with it whatever food and supplies the man had.

Clint, realizing he was out in the open with the canteen, stooped and picked up his gun, and then turned and ran for a nearby alley. As he entered the alley, he heard two bullets slam into the side of the building, either deliberately missing or fired in haste.

In the alley he holstered his gun and greedily drank from the canteen.

The killer was livid. Whoever the man had been, he had managed to get his canteen to Adams before the killer could stop him. That meant that Adams now had water, but at least the man's horse had spooked and run off. That meant that Adams would not be able to claim whatever supplies the man might have had in his saddlebags, nor would he be able to get the man's rifle.

Still, with a canteen full of water, Adams would no longer be suffering from thirst. The killer didn't know how much good the water would do Adams's hunger pains, but part of his plan had been for Adams to suffer from hunger *and* thirst.

For the first time, something had gone very wrong.

TWENTY-THREE

In the alley Clint hefted the canteen. It was more than half full, and as much as he wanted to guzzle the water from it, he took several more small sips and then replaced the top. This water might have to last a long time.

In his haste to quench his thirst, Clint had completely ignored the fact that the stranger was lying in the street . . . dead . . . he thought.

Jesus, he thought, what if he wasn't dead? He couldn't just leave the man out there, especially since it was his fault he'd gotten shot in the first place. If Clint hadn't been so mistrustful he could have hustled the man under cover and then questioned him. Instead, he'd made the man sit out there in the open on his horse, as big a target as he could be. The killer had probably seen the man getting ready to give Clint the canteen and had killed him to try to stop him. Clint tried not to think about what kind of food was in the man's saddlebags. The horse *and* the saddlebags were long gone now.

The man, however, was still lying in the street, and if he was alive, Clint had to get him under cover and treat his wounds. He couldn't go out there, though, until it was completely dark, and that time was not so very far away.

He crawled to the mouth of the alley and sneaked a look at the street. He could see the man's legs, but not much else.

"Hey, mister." He kept his voice low for fear the killer would hear him.

The prone stranger did not answer. Perhaps he hadn't heard Clint, either.

"Hey . . . mister!"

Still no answer.

"Mister, you alive? Move your legs if you are."

Nothing. He was either dead, unconscious, or he just couldn't hear.

Clint withdrew his head and sat with his back to the wall. He'd just have to wait a little while, until it was dark, and then he'd be able to go and check on the man himself. While he did that, he'd also be able to check the man's pockets. He might be carrying something Clint could use.

Clint wondered what the killer was doing now. Was he also waiting for darkness to fall? Did he intend to come down and check on the man, too?

It occurred to Clint that if he just stayed where he was he might get his first look at the killer. Still, if he did that and the man was alive, he'd truly be responsible for his death. No, he was going to have to take the chance and satisfy himself that the man was either alive and in need of help, or dead.

If the man was alive, he hoped he would be able to last another fifteen or twenty minutes. . . .

The killer watched the street. The man lying there was not moving. The killer felt sure he was dead.

Adams, on the other hand, could be anywhere. He had probably found himself a hole to hide in while he drank all the water in the canteen. No, the Gun-smith was too smart for that. He'd probably nurse his newfound water supply. At least the killer had kept the dead man from giving Adams any food.

He wondered idly who the man was. Probably just a drifter looking for someplace to spend the night. The killer smiled, then laughed. He bet that when the man rode into town he had no idea he'd be spending the rest of his life there.

It took seventeen minutes for darkness to fall com-pletely, but to Clint it felt like hours. And what about that poor bastard lying in the street? If he was still alive, how long had it seemed to him?

Clint left the canteen on the ground in the alley and slid out into the street on his belly. He didn't know where the killer was now, but hopefully he wouldn't be spotted until it was too late.

He crawled on his belly, moving closer and closer to the downed man, until he was able to reach out and touch the man's leg. He'd touched dead men before, and that's all it took for him to realize that the man was dead. He moved closer, until he was lying on the ground right next to the man. The face was turned toward him, and he could plainly see now that he was dead.

"Sorry," he whispered to the man. Sorry he'd gotten him killed, and sorry he was now going to have to go through the dead man's pockets.

He didn't find anything in the man's pants pockets. The man was wearing a gunbelt, but his gun was out in the center of the street somewhere. Clint couldn't see it from where he was, and he had no intention of trying to find it. Finally he checked the man's shirt pocket, and that was where he found the treasure. He had to roll the man partially over to get to it, but when he saw what was in the pocket, he had to stifle a cry of pleasure.

In his hand was the most beautiful piece of hardtack he'd ever seen.

The killer looked out the window and thought he saw something. There wasn't much of a moon out, and there was no light to see by, but he prided himself on his excellent night vision.

He squinted, staring down at the street. He could see the dead man but nothing else.

Wait: Was there something else moving out there?

Sonofabitch! Was that Adams, crawling toward the body in the street? What did he think he could get from the body that would help him? Another gun? Another gun was no good to him if he couldn't see anything to shoot at. The man's horse was gone, and if he had any food it had been in his saddlebags.

Look at him! The legendary Gunsmith, crawling on his belly!

The killer raised his rifle and sighted down the barrel, but he didn't fire. The fact that Clint Adams was crawling on his belly in the street like a snake showed how desperate he had become.

Let him crawl. Let him reach the dead man and find nothing to help him.

Let him humiliate himself.

Clint clutched his treasure to his chest and crawled back into the alley. He wondered if the killer had watched him crawl back and forth on his belly. If he had, he had probably gotten a lot of satisfaction out of it. He also probably figured that Clint wouldn't find anything on the body that would help him.

The killer had been wrong and, somehow, that was encouraging.

TWENTY-FOUR

Clint found a back door that he could force, and he went inside. He closed the door behind him, then found a couple of wooden crates to pile up against it. If the killer tried to enter, the crates would fall over and warn him.

He found a table with three legs, and a barrel. He left the table alone and moved the barrel over near a crate, which he sat on.

The only other thing he'd found on the body was a box of lucifer matches. He made sure to take it with him.

He spread his treasure out on the barrelhead, then took one match out and struck it. In the flickering light offered by the flame he stared at the piece of hardtack, and the canteen. He picked up the dried meat, shook the match until the flame went out, and then took a bite. It was the first bit of food he'd had in days, and to him it was as delicious as any meal he'd ever had in a fancy restaurant. He chewed the hard biscuit, savoring it, then uncapped the canteen and took a small sip of water. He slipped the rest of the hardtack into his shirt pocket, then capped the canteen. He'd had his dinner, and in the morning he'd have a similar breakfast. Now it was time to get some sleep. In the morning the game would start again, but he was tired of being the hunted.

Maybe tomorrow he could start a new game.

Rick Hartman was worried about Clint Adams. Before Clint left he promised Rick that he'd send him a telegram when he reached the town of Patience. Rick was curious to find out who had sent Clint the message to meet there. Clint must have reached Patience by now, and it wasn't like him not to keep his word.

Rick rolled over in bed and looked down at the woman sleeping next to him. Like his friend Clint, Rick loved women, in all shapes and sizes. His preference, however, ran to tall, willowy women with long, slender legs and good, solid breasts. This woman, Glenda, had been working for him for a month now. She was about five-eight and had masses of blond hair that hung down past her shoulders. Her mouth was wide, the lower lip twice as full as the upper. It was that lush lower lip that he had first noticed when she came in to apply for a job, and then he had slowly taken in the rest of her. He had been impressed not only with her beauty—which was undeniable—but also with the way she carried herself, so proud and erect, with grace and poise.

She was lying on her back now, with the sheet covering one breast, the left one. Although she had small breasts, they were round and firm, just the way he liked them. The right one was bare, and he reached over and touched the rosy-colored nipple with his finger. She had the most responsive nipples he had ever seen on a woman. She moaned, and her tongue flicked out to lick her bottom lip. He leaned over her and circled the nipple with the tip of his tongue, licking her smooth, creamy skin before touching it directly. She groaned again, and the nipple tightened. He opened his mouth to take as much of her breast into it as he could. Her hands came up to cup the back of his head while his hand moved down over her smooth, flat belly and delved into her wiry pubic patch to find her already moist and ready. He slipped one finger inside her wet warmth, and she groaned and moved her hips. One of *her* hands now moved down between them to take hold of his hard, erect penis and stroke it lovingly.

As he rolled over to move atop her, she moaned again and reached for him. She wrapped him up in her arms and long legs, and he slid into her easily.

Later, he thought, he'd try sending a telegram to Patience, Oklahoma.

"Are you sure about that?" Rick asked the telegraph clerk.

"I'm positive, Mr. Hartman," the little man said earnestly. "There just ain't an active key in Patience, Oklahoma."

Rick frowned. It would certainly explain why Clint hadn't sent a telegram as he had promised, but Rick felt uncomfortable with the information.

"What's the nearest town to Patience that does have a key?"

"I'd have to check on that."

"Well, check it," Rick said firmly, "and get back to me as soon as you know." He fixed the man with a hard stare and added, "This is very important to me."

"Sure, Mr. Hartman," the clerk said. "I'll let you know as soon as I know."

"All right."

Rick left the telegraph office and paused on the boardwalk outside. If Clint was in trouble and couldn't get word to him, what was he going to do? Patience was just too damn far away for him to go himself. He was going to have to find someone who was within spitting distance of that town and get that person over there to check it out as soon as possible.

TWENTY-FIVE

When Clint woke he had a bad moment when he didn't know where he was. For a moment, he thought he was still in that deserted saloon, sitting on the floor behind the bar, feverish, having dreamed most of what had happened over the past day or so.

He sat up straight and looked around him. It was dark, but there was some light coming in from outside. Slowly he drew his wits in about him and came back to the present.

He'd been dreaming again, the way he had when he *was* sitting in the saloon. Feverish. He'd been dreaming about Bill Hickok. . . .

Clint Adams had not been in Deadwood when Hickok was killed, but in his dream he was there. He was standing at the bar, watching Hickok play poker, when the coward Jack McCall came in.

Hickok, intent on his poker hand, was unaware that McCall was there. Initially, McCall circled the table, probably trying to summon up the courage to do what he had come to do. Clint watched McCall, and he *knew* what McCall was going to do. He wanted to warn Hickok but found that he could not move, and he could not speak. All he could do was watch in horror as McCall stopped behind Hickok, drew a gun from inside his coat, pointed it at the back of Hickok's head, and fired.

The bullet impacted in slow motion. Clint saw Hickok's head jerk on his shoulders from the blow. The cards fell from his nerveless fingers, fluttering to the floor. They fell, so slowly that Clint actually saw them land, one at a time . . . and then Hickok was falling sideways from his chair, also slowly . . . ever so slowly . . . until his body struck the floor. He didn't even bounce, just struck the floor and lay there, still, so still . . .

. . . And then, in his dream, Hickok's face turned up toward him, blood streaming from his nose, his mouth, his eyes. . . .

That was when he woke up. He was sweating now, but he knew it was from the dream, not from any fever.

He wiped his hand across his face and then went for that precious piece of hardtack he had in his pocket. He decided to go ahead and finish it for breakfast. There was no point in saving any for lunch, when he might not even live that long.

He washed it down with a couple of mouthsful of warm water, then stopped up the canteen. The water he would save. There was too much for him to drink all at once, anyway.

Slowly, he got to his feet. The hardtack and water had helped, but he still felt very weak from lack of proper nourishment. He walked to the back door and removed the crates he had piled there. When he opened the door he stood frozen for a moment in the shaft of light, then struggled through it until he was outside. He stood, just letting his senses adjust. He had never had such difficulty waking up before, and he knew it was because of his undernourished condition.

He took deep breaths and finally started to feel alert and aware. The sense of danger returned, and he realized he was out in the open. He looked around, telling himself that while his assailant could be anywhere in town, the same was true of him. What were the chances of their running into each other by accident?

This had to end today, he told himself. He didn't know if he could last much longer than that. In the beginning, the assailant had a huge advantage over him. Since then Clint had been able to narrow the distance between them somewhat, but the longer this stretched out, the more the advantage swung in favor of the other man again.

He took out his gun and checked it, making sure it was fully loaded and in proper working order. Satisfied that it was, he tried to decide what his next move should be. Actually, there was only one possible move. Somewhere in this town there was a man who wanted desperately to kill him. The cat-and-mouse game was probably over. The next time they encountered each other, the killer would probably try his best to finish it.

Clint had to make sure that *he* found the other man first.

The killer had slept fitfully. Adams was loose, and he had no idea where he was. All he could think of all night long was that when daylight came he was going to have to find the Gunsmith and finish this thing for good. There wasn't time for any more games. The longer he let it go on now, the more chance there was that Adams would find some way out of town. The killer had gone to too much trouble to set this up to let Adams get away now.

Adams had to die today, so that the killer could stamp his debt paid.

● ● ●

Sam Fulton had been in the town of Boylston, Oklahoma, for about a week, and he and the town seemed to have worn out their welcome with each other. Some of that was due to the lady lying next to him. She was the pretty wife of one of the town's leading citizens, and she was more interested in Sam Fulton than she was in her husband. That was why Fulton didn't mind receiving the telegram from Rick Hartman asking him to go to Patience.

Randi Taylor rolled over in bed, and the sheet slipped off of her hip. Every time she moved, it slid off farther, revealing more and more of her. The hip was the last part of her that had been covered, and now she was completely naked. Looking down at her, Fulton thought that maybe he could have used a few more days here, but with the telegram from Hartman, he would have had to leave, anyway.

Randi was a blousy, big-breasted blonde married to a man twice her age—and *she* was no spring chicken. Fulton figured her for thirty-five, maybe more. Still, she was full-bodied and had a lot of energy and no inhibitions when it came to sex.

He reached over and stroked her hip. She moaned in her sleep and rolled onto her back. Her big breasts flattened out on her chest, the nipples soft and pink. He reached over and stroked her right breast, and the nipple sprang to life at his touch. He kept his hand there.

Fulton was a medium-sized man in his thirties who had spent the past ten years just traveling, and seeing the country at his leisure. He was more than competent with a gun, while not known for his handling of one. In fact, he wasn't particularly well known for anything, which suited him just fine.

Randi wiggled her hips and opened her eyes. When

she saw Fulton, she smiled and reached over her head to stretch. He watched her body grow taut and then relax.

"Mornin'," she said.

"Good mornin'," he said, sliding his hand down over her belly.

She moved her hips again as he stroked her until she was moist.

Fulton didn't know Clint Adams, but he knew that Hartman and Adams were friends. Fulton was one of dozens of men who acted as eyes and ears throughout the West for Hartman, who did "favors" for the saloon owner, for which he paid them a fee.

There would be no fee, though, for this ride to Patience. Hartman seemed to feel that Adams might be in real danger, so Fulton agreed to check it out.

This time it *was* a favor.

"Um," she said, closing her eyes, "do you really have to leave today?"

"Yes," he said, sliding one leg over her, "I really do—but not for an hour or so."

TWENTY-SIX

Clint stayed to the back of the buildings on his side of the street and worked his way as far as he could. In a couple of places he had to scale some wooden fences, and found he had to rest afterward. Finally he had worked his way back to the end of town where the burned-out livery stable was. Surely the killer would not think to look for him there.

Clint needed a secure place from which to watch the main street. Hidden behind the burned-out husk of the stable, he could look right down the main street. Now all he had to do was outwait the killer. Whoever it was had to become impatient enough to come out into the street to try to find Clint.

He only hoped that the man was more impatient than he was.

The killer stared down at the main street. It was going to happen there, he thought. Right down there. There were only two ways to find Adams now. One, he could stay right where he was and wait for him to show himself, but the chances were good that Adams was doing the same thing. That left the second choice, which was to show himself, thereby drawing Adams out.

Yes, that was it. . . .

He smiled. Maybe the game-playing wasn't over after all.

Clint was sitting on the ground, hidden from view but with a clear view of the street. He knew this might take hours, but he told himself that he had to be patient. It was still early morning, and the chances of the killer showing himself—

He stopped his thoughts short as he saw something. He squinted, as the sun was in his eyes, but yes, there was definitely someone standing in the street. The figure was in the center of the street, standing stock still. It appeared to be a man, and he was armed. He held a rifle in one hand and a pistol in the other, and he was just standing there.

This was his first look at his assailant, his *tormentor,* and he couldn't even make out who it was!

Hastily, he got to his feet and moved away from the rubble. He lifted a hand to shield his eyes but still could not make out the face of the man. Suddenly the man holstered his gun, lifted his hand, and saluted Clint, then turned and walked away.

"Wait!" Clint shouted. Even though he knew he was wrong, he started to run. With mounting anxiety he realized this might be his only look at the man, his only chance to catch him . . . and he started running harder. . . .

The killer smiled to himself as he saluted Adams and then turned and walked away. When he knew he was hidden from Adams's view, he broke into a run, down an alley. He ran to the end of it and stopped there to wait.

By setting himself up as the mouse, being chased by the cat, he was actually becoming the cat once again.

• • •

Clint ran down the main street until he reached the point where he figured the man had been standing. He had to regain control of himself, but his heart was pounding so hard. . . .

He looked around and saw an alley. That had to be where the man had gone. He started to run, then deliberately slowed down. That was what the assailant wanted. Instead of Clint drawing him out, the man had drawn *him* out by revealing himself. He *wanted* Clint to chase him.

Clint stopped at the mouth of the alley. If he went in, he would be playing right into the assailant's hands. Yet, if he didn't go, when would he get another chance to catch him? At least this way they were both on the ground.

He took a deep breath and entered the alley.

The killer heard Clint Adams come into the alley and waited until he was halfway down, then turned and kicked over a barrel. Grinning, he turned and ran along the back of the buildings. His clear advantage now was that he knew every inch of this town. He had mapped it out on paper and had then memorized it. He could negotiate its streets and alleys at night, if he had to.

And maybe that's just what he'd do.

Clint stopped when he heard something fall and roll, probably a barrel. Sure enough, there it was, rolling toward him, but without much velocity. He easily side-stepped it and then ignored it. If he turned to follow its progress, his back would be an easy target. Even though he felt that this assailant wouldn't shoot him in the back even if he had the chance, there was no sense in tempting him.

He waited a few minutes, listening intently, and thought he heard the sound of retreating footsteps. Quickly, he moved to the back of the alley and out to where he stood behind the buildings. It was as if he had just stepped out of that dark room a couple of hours earlier. He looked both ways, trying to figure out a way to go, when he heard the sound of a door slamming to his right. Slowly he moved in that direction until he found a door that was ajar. Instead of going into the building, he took a few steps back and looked at it. It was a two-story wooden structure. From this end it could have been anything—a saloon, a hotel, a feed and grain, anything.

He moved to the door again and listened. Inside he could hear footsteps on a wooden floor, and maybe on some wooden steps.

There was a low roof above him, which would give him access to the second floor without going into the building from here. He looked around, found a barrel, and set it against the back wall. He stepped atop the barrel and reached up to grasp the edge of the roof. For a moment he hung there, without the strength to pull himself up, but then he steeled himself and slowly scaled the side of the wall until he was lying on that low roof, trying to catch his breath. He realized that he was an easy target, but he just had to take a few seconds to regain his wind.

Once he was able to breathe almost normally, he rolled over, got to his feet, and walked over to a window. He was able to slide his fingertips underneath and raise the window so he could climb inside. Once inside, he saw what looked like all the other hotel rooms he'd ever been in, only this one was bare, except for a fallen bed frame with no mattress. There were pale spaces on the floor where some other furniture used to stand.

He walked across the room to the door, which was
ajar. He listened intently, then slowly opened the door
and looked out into the hall. He slid his gun from
his holster and eased out into the hallway. Standing
still, he listened again, wondering if the assailant was
downstairs, up here with him in one of the rooms, or not
even in the building anymore. When he heard footsteps
above him, he had his answer.

The man was up on the roof.

The killer stood still on the roof, then walked across
it again. He made just enough noise to tell Clint Adams
that he was there. He knew Adams would come up. It
would be so easy just to stay here and wait for him.

Stay, wait, and kill him.

TWENTY-SEVEN

The roof was empty.

Clint had found the room with the roof hatch, and when he climbed up he took a deep breath and stuck his head out the hatch, where it could be easily shot off. He looked around, and the roof was empty. He climbed up and walked first to the front, then to the back. There was a low roof at both, where the assailant could have dropped down. There were also rooftops on both sides, where he could have gone. The roof on his right was lower, the one on the left higher, but both were accessible. He was trying to make up his mind which way to go when the shot came.

There was no cover on the roof, so the only thing he could do as a second bullet embedded itself in the roof at his feet was throw himself over the side. He was standing closest to the front, so he ran and dove over. When he hit the low roof he grunted, then rolled. The roof was slanted and he started to lose control, and then suddenly a portion of it went out from beneath him. He fell through, was suspended for a moment in thin air, and then hit the ground hard.

He didn't remember hitting the ground, though, because when he did, everything went black.

• • •

From the higher roof the killer fired a third shot and then laughed as Clint Adams dove off the roof. The killer dropped down to the hotel roof and moved to the front so he could look down. He saw the hole in the slanted roof and knew that Adams had fallen through. He laughed, replaced the spent shells in his pistol with live ones, and holstered it. Carefully, he lowered himself to the slanted roof, but as he worked his way to the hole, he saw Adams starting to move. He had intended to drop down and take Adams's gun away, but the Gunsmith was already regaining consciousness. If the killer dropped down now, he might have to kill Adams quickly—and he wanted Adams to suffer first.

Feeling in control of the situation again, he climbed back onto the hotel roof and waited for Clint Adams to regain his senses.

Clint started to move even before he opened his eyes. It was instinct, self-preservation. He was on his hands and knees when he finally opened his eyes. Something felt wet on his shirt, and for a moment he thought he'd been shot. When he looked, though, he saw that he had fallen on his canteen, breaking it. He slid it off his shoulder and shook it. There was probably a mouthful of water left. He pushed himself into the hotel doorway and drained the canteen, tossing it aside. He looked up at the hole he'd fallen through and had to laugh at himself. Why not? The assailant had probably laughed himself silly, watching him throw himself off the roof and then fall through to the ground. He probed his ribs and legs and shook out his arms, satisfying himself that he was still in one piece.

"Adams!"

His head jerked up at the sound of the voice.

"Clint Adams! Are you all right? Did you break anything?"

Clint didn't answer. He wanted the man to keep talking. From what he had heard so far, he could not identify him.

"Come on, Clint, talk to me!" the voice called. "I know you're all right!"

Clint frowned, trying to identify the voice, but he just couldn't.

"Who are you?" he finally asked.

"Ah," the voice called, "that's the burning question, isn't it?"

Clint waited a moment, then asked, "Are you going to answer it?"

"Sure I am," the man said, "as soon as you catch me. Come on, Adams. I'm waiting up here for you, only this time do yourself a favor: Use the stairs."

TWENTY-EIGHT

Clint sat there, running the man's voice over and over in his mind, but no matter how many times he replayed it, he couldn't identify the voice. It seemed that the only way to identify the assailant was going to be by catching him.

He stood up and checked his gun, to make sure it hadn't been damaged by the fall. It looked all right, but the real test would come when he fired it.

Hopefully that would be very soon.

He turned to go into the hotel and use the stairs, but stopped short. Instead, he walked to the next building, which had at one time been a hardware store. This was the building where the roof was lower, but accessible to the roof of the hotel. He tried the door and found it locked. By putting his shoulder and weight into it, he managed to snap the door open with a minimum of noise. He went inside and closed the door behind him. Since he had broken it, it stood ajar.

Inside, he looked around. There were tools littered about, old tools that had rusted. The shelving had fallen down long ago and lay on the floor in pieces. In the back he saw a doorway, which led to a hallway, which in turn led to the stairway to the second floor. He went up the stairs and discovered that there were three rooms there, all bare. In the ceiling of one of them he found the roof hatch. He had to go downstairs to get a crate to stand on so he could reach the hatch. Once he was on the roof he stayed low and hurried over to the hotel roof. He remained low for a few moments, then stood up, his gun extended in front of him. As he had expected, there was no one on the roof.

He climbed up onto the hotel roof, alert for a repeat of what had happened just a little while ago. He watched the higher roof across from him carefully as he catwalked his way over to it. He flattened his back against the wall of the higher building, holding his gun at shoulder level. If the assailant was on the higher roof, then this thing was going to end one way or another right now . . . but he doubted it.

The only way he was going to get onto the higher roof was to holster his gun, jump up, and catch the edge with both hands. Once he did that he would be in a very vulnerable position—but no more vulnerable than moments after he had fallen through that low roof.

Well, there was no other way to do this, so he holstered the gun, jumped up, and grabbed onto the edge of the roof. He pulled himself up, digging his toes into the wall, and finally rolled over onto the higher roof. He pulled his gun quickly, but there was no need. There was no one on this roof, either.

He sat there on the roof, looking around. The hatch cover into the building was off, lying next to the open hatch. That didn't necessarily mean that the assailant had gone down through it.

He stood up and walked to the other end of the roof. The nearest building was eight feet away. A long-legged man might have made the jump, but Clint wasn't in any shape to try it.

That left the hatch.

He turned and walked to the hatch, looking down into the roof below. The assailant must have been laughing his head off. He had Clint wondering if he wasn't waiting in that room below, waiting until Clint stuck his head through, so he could chop it off.

Clint stood next to the open hatch, crossed his hands over his chest—still holding his gun—then took a step and dropped through.

When he hit the floor it jarred his ankles, even though he bent at the knees to try to absorb the impact. He covered the room with his gun, turning left and right, and turning completely around. The room was empty. There weren't even any marks on the floor to indicate that it had once been furnished. Clint kept his gun ready and approached the closed door. He tried the knob and found that the door was locked. He pressed his ear to the door but couldn't hear anything outside. The assailant probably thought it was pretty funny, locking him in there that way. Clint felt like he was chasing the man through a maze. It was frustrating, to say the least.

Clint tried the door again, but it was no use. It was locked tight. Now he had two choices: He could shoot the lock, or he could go out the window. The window would be quieter, so he walked to it and looked out. There was no low roof outside, and no ledge. It was a sheer drop to the street. He could probably make the drop without injuring himself, but that would be bucking the odds. So far he'd fallen through a roof and dropped through a hatch without hurting himself.

Why push his luck?

He walked to the door and fired two shots at the lock, which splintered. He replaced the two spent shells in the gun before opening the door. He flattened himself against the wall next to the door, counted to ten, then quickly stepped out into the hall. He swung left and right with his gun, but there was no one there.

It was a short hall, not like the hallway in the hotel. He still couldn't tell what this building might have been. He made his way to one end of the hall, and when he didn't find a stairway, moved to the other end, where he did find one. It appeared to lead to the back of the building. He went down the stairs carefully, his gun ready, and at the base came to a door. Not surprisingly, that door was locked, also. More games from his assailant.

Instead of shooting off the lock, Clint turned to his right. There was another short hall, which led to a cur- tained doorway. The curtain was dusty and tattered. As he pushed it aside he could smell the dust. Now he was in a room with a large window that looked out onto the main street. He was in what was once some kind of a store, but he couldn't tell what kind.

He crossed to the front door and tried it. It was also locked. There was no way of knowing which way the assailant had gone out. With the front, however, he could tell that the man wasn't waiting just on the other side. He decided that he would go out the front. This time, however, he did not waste any bullets. Two well- placed kicks splintered the doorjamb, and he opened the door and stepped outside.

He stayed in the doorway for a few moments, waiting to see if the assailant would give him a clue about which way to go next. The man seemed to be enjoying what Clint had come to think of as their own little game of hide-and-go-seek.

He himself, on the other hand, wasn't enjoying it one bit.

TWENTY-NINE

The killer *was* enjoying himself.

At one point he had actually found himself grinning broadly, almost laughing out loud as he led Clint Adams on a merry chase.

The whole thing reminded him of something years ago. . . .

The killer remembered when he was a child, watching the other kids playing games, running around with grins on their faces. Laughing and shouting while he watched from the window. What did they have to be so happy about? he'd wondered back then. They were all living in that home together, either having no parents, or parents who had put them there to get rid of them.

Of course, they wouldn't have let him play even if he wanted to. His father was a killer, they said. They didn't want to play with the son of a killer.

Watching them, running and laughing, he wanted to kill them all. *His* father was different in one way: He had put his son in this home only because he couldn't drag him around the country with him—not and do the kind of work he did. He sent money to the orphanage, though, and stopped to visit every time he was nearby.

The killer knew that—secretly, deep down inside— when his father came to visit him the other kids were

envious. The watched with wide eyes, awed by the tall
man dressed in black. They stayed away from him while
his father was there and didn't dare tease him. After
his father left, though, the teasing would start. After
the first few fights—some of which he won, some of
which he lost—he decided the it wasn't worth fighting
over. From that time on he just kept his own distance,
stayed away from everyone else, and knew that when
he got old enough he'd leave. His father would take
him and would teach him how to use a gun, and once
he knew that, no one would tease him ever again.

Only his father never did take him out of that home.
That was because Clint Adams had killed him. So the
killer left on his own, picked up a gun, and taught
himself how to use it. He had a lifetime of vengeance
ahead of him, but the first one to feel it was going to
be the man they called the Gunsmith.

Clint Adams was only the first installment on all the
debts he had to pay back. The way he felt now, he only
hoped they would all taste as sweet as this.

Sam Fulton was camped a full day's ride from the
town of Patience. He had made pretty good time since
leaving Boylston. He had contacted Hartman once along
the way, just to see if anything had turned up on Adams.
Hartman assured him it hadn't and that he was even
more worried than ever about Clint Adams. Fulton
assured him he'd find out for sure.

Of course, if Fulton arrived in Patience and found no
one there, tracking Clint Adams down was not going to
be easy. It would all depend on whether he had *ever*
been there and whether he'd left a trail.

Fulton poured himself another cup of coffee. If he
got to Patience and found Adams, it would be the first

time he'd ever met a man of Adams's reputation. He was looking forward to meeting the man behind the legend.

Rick Hartman had received one telegram from Sam Fulton since Fulton left the town of Boylston. Sitting in his saloon, watching as business boomed yet another night, his fear that something had happened to Clint Adams was growing, almost unchecked.

He wished he could ride to Patience himself, but it would take him too long to get there to do any good. He was going to have to sit tight patiently while Sam Fulton found out what, if anything, had happened to Clint Adams.

THIRTY

Clint Adams stepped out of the building, onto the boardwalk, not knowing quite what to expect. The assailant had certainly changed his tack. Instead of sitting back and forcing Clint to make all the moves, he had suddenly become much more aggressive. Perhaps he felt he was losing control of the situation, and this was his way of taking control back. If that was his intention, he had certainly done so. Clint had to figure that at the moment he was in the assailant's sights.

The assailant had had more than his share of chances to kill Clint today. Clint knew what he himself was capable of, and thought the man foolish not to have done so by now. Every time he let Clint out of his sights, he was giving Clint a chance to come back with some sort of offensive of his own.

The assailant was playing with fire.

The killer watched as Clint stepped out of the building onto the street. Leading Adams through the deserted town and the empty buildings had been exhilarating, and he didn't want that feeling to fade. He could have killed Adams where he stood now, but he decided against it. He *knew* the kind of fire he was playing with, he *knew* what Clint Adams was capable of . . . and that made it even more enjoyable. This was living on the edge, the way his father had lived most of his life.

What the killer didn't know was that his father would have taken the first opportunity to kill Clint Adams, and gotten the job done. His father was a *professional* killer, something that *this* killer could not yet claim to be.

All in all, that was probably Clint Adams's biggest advantage.

Clint decided that his assailant had had enough time to kill him while he was standing there, if that was what he wanted to do. He stepped down from the boardwalk into the street and holstered his gun.

"Are the games over?" he shouted.

No answer.

"Why don't you just come out into the street and we'll finish it."

That drew a laugh and then a reply.

"You'd like that, wouldn't you, Adams?" the assailant called out. Clint tried to pinpoint the location of the voice, but in the empty street of a dead town, it echoed and could have come from anywhere.

"That would be doing things your way, wouldn't it?" the assailant called out. "But we're here to do things my way, isn't that right?"

"And what's your way?"

Another laugh, and then the man called out, "You'll see, Adams. You'll see."

Clint waited a few moments, but there were no further statements from the assailant. Apparently he was going to give Clint some time to think things over.

Clint crossed over to the other side of the street and walked back in the direction of the burned-out livery. When he came to a likely-looking storefront, he stopped and stepped inside. What were the chances that he was walking into the same building the assailant was in? That would be too much of a coincidence, and Clint Adams didn't believe in coincidence.

This storefront was much like the others, littered with debris. There was a barrel that he was able to upright and sit on.

Since the assailant was giving him this time, he decided to make the best use of it he could.

First, he played the man's voice over and over in his mind. Although he couldn't identify it, the voice itself sounded like it came from the East. To a certain extent, it sounded educated. Also, it would have taken an intelligent mind to set all of this up. Closing his eyes tightly, the voice sounded to him like a young man's voice. The assailant was in his twenties. If that was the case, that would rule out the assailant being an old enemy. The man was simply too young for that. What could this young man have against him, then, unless . . . unless his hunger for vengeance had nothing to do with himself, but with someone else. A relative? A father, perhaps?

Clint abandoned the voice for the moment and now went to the only look he'd had at the man. Standing in the street that way, he'd only given Clint what amounted to a silhouette to identify him by.

Back when it had happened, there had been something familiar about the man, only Clint had been too anxious to catch him to concentrate on it. Now he tried to conjure up the vision of the man standing in the center of the street. He still could not make out the man's features, but he realized that there had been something familiar about the way the man had stood. He was a tall man, and Clint thought he had been wearing black. A tall man clad in black, with something familiar in the way he was standing . . .

It was in the back of Clint's mind, in the recesses of his memory, and he couldn't bring it to the surface. The important thing, however, was that it *was* there. Given time, he would be able to bring it to the surface and maybe—finally—identify the man who was playing games with him and who would eventually try to kill him.

THIRTY-ONE

Clint came awake with a start. Somehow, sitting on that barrel, he had fallen asleep. Once again his physical condition—never having improved all *that* much because of the hardtack and water—was deteriorating. He felt weak and somewhat dizzy and—having just awakened—more than a little disoriented.

He stood and rubbed his hands over his face. He walked to the window and looked out. He hadn't realized it earlier, but from here he could see the dead man, still lying in the street. If he could only locate the man's horse, there might be more food in the saddlebags. Maybe even another canteen. Clint touched his lips, which felt dry.

What must Rick Hartman be thinking right now? he wondered. It had been days since Clint had contacted Rick. Surely his friend would be worried by now. What would he do? He certainly wouldn't try to travel all the way to Patience himself. No, he'd try to find someone nearby whom he could send to look. Yeah, knowing Rick, that was what he'd do, and that meant that help was on the way. If Clint could just stay in hiding until it arrived . . . but that wasn't really Clint Adams's style. Everything in him rebelled at the idea of hiding, especially now that he almost had the assailant's identity figured out.

He closed his eyes and conjured up the vision once again of the man standing in the street. Someone, somewhere in his past had looked exactly like that when he stood. If only he could remember . . .

He had stood opposite many men in his life—so many of them, in fact, that they ran together in his mind. He was sad to say that he didn't remember every man he had killed in a face-to-face confrontation. He felt that anyone who killed a man should remember that for as long as *he* went on living, but it didn't always work that way. Not when you were a man with a reputation, not when other men with guns wanted nothing more than to kill you.

Clint tried to sort through the names and faces in his memory but couldn't quite bring the one he wanted to the surface.

There were other factors to consider, though. He turned away from the window, walked back to the barrel, and sat down to consider them.

There were all the other bodies that the assailant—or killer—had left littered around town. He had killed them to make a point. Why would the man have chosen Katy Littlefeather and Sandy Spillane, among Clint's friends, to taunt him with look-alikes? He could understand the Masterson look-alike. He and Masterson were well known as friends. The killer wanted Clint to know what it felt like to lose someone close to him.

But why choose these women?

Clint had worked with the three lady bounty hunters many times, both together and individually. What if this killer was the son, or relative, of someone he had helped the ladies track down?

And finally, the man popped to the surface of Clint's

consciousness. It was someone that all four of them had been involved in tracking down, but it was Clint who had killed him.

Could that be the answer? Could this young man be *that* man's son?

Clint closed his eyes and, sure enough, the man standing in the street here in Patience bore a strong resemblance—just in the way he stood—to that man Clint had killed years ago.

If this was the case, it was a first in the life of Clint Adams.

A son had come back to avenge his father.

THIRTY-TWO

Looking out the window, Clint saw that it was about an hour shy of dusk. He had to make some kind of move to assure that the killer didn't know where he was. That meant finding a back way out. He looked around and saw a doorway in the back wall. It probably led to a storeroom. He went through the doorway and found that the room was darker than the front. That was due to the fact that the windows back here were covered. There were two small windows in the back wall, covered by old, dusty curtains. He walked to them one at a time and tore the curtains off. What was left of the light outside streamed in and he saw that there was no back door.

"Shit," he said. He was going to have to try to climb out one of the small windows.

He looked around for something to break the windows with, something that might muffle the sound of the breaking glass. He stopped short when he saw something in a corner of the room.

There was a cot there, and something that looked human was lying on it.

Jesus, he thought, don't let it be another dead body. Having discovered Sandy Spillane, Katy Littlefeather, and Bat Masterson doubles, this one figured to be an Anne Archer double. That being the case, he especially didn't want to find her dead.

Slowly he walked to the cot and, sure enough, the figure lying on it looked feminine. She was lying with her back to him, her knees drawn up. He reached for her once, pulled back his hand, then shook his head at himself.

Holding his breath, afraid of what he would see, he reached her shoulder to turn her over. How would he have killed this one? A slit throat? A bullet in the heart, or the head?

He touched her shoulder and was surprised to find it warm. He had probably killed her very recently. He turned her over then, and when her face came into view he started with shock.

Her eyes were wide open, staring at him with naked terror. The cords in her neck stood out, and her mouth was set in a grimace behind a tight gag. Her hands and feet were also tightly bound. From the looks of her she must have been lying there for a long time like that.

Thank God, he thought, she was still alive.

THIRTY-THREE

He untied her hands, and she quickly used them to push herself farther away from him. She was still staring at him with fear.

"Take it easy," he said. "I'm not going to hurt you."

She watched as he untied her legs. She must have been very thirsty. He was sorry he had no water to offer her.

"How long have you been here?"

She frowned, then opened her mouth to speak, only nothing came out. She frowned again, cleared her throat, tried to use her tongue to moisten her lips, and tried again to speak.

"You're not . . . not with . . . him?"

"No," he said. "I'm a victim, like you are."

"Who is he?" she asked. "What does he want?"

She was pretty underneath the dirt on her face. She did not resemble Anne Archer, though, not from the front. She was more slender than Anne, younger, not as full-breasted. Still, he couldn't help notice that she was pretty.

"I'll have to explain that later," he said. "Didn't you hear me in the other room? Why didn't you try to call out, or make some kind of noise to let me know you were back here?"

"I . . . I thought it was him."

"Can you stand?"

"I don't know."

"Try now."

She slid to the edge of the cot and put her feet down on the floor. When she tried to stand she fell, and he caught her.

"Easy," he said. She must have been here, without food and water, even longer than he. "Listen," he said, "we've got to get out of here. Right now he knows we're in here. We've got to find someplace else to hide, and talk."

"I'll try."

"Has he fed you at all?"

She nodded.

"He gave me food and water for a while, but not for days."

"Did you see the others?"

"What others?"

"He had . . . others here in town, also as prisoners," Clint said.

"Where are they?"

"I'm sorry," he said, "but they're all dead."

She gasped and said, "He kept saying he was going to kill me."

"Well, we're not going to give him the chance," he said. "Come on."

She took a step, but her legs wouldn't hold her.

"I can't," she said. "You go, save yourself."

He smiled at her and said, "We're going together, or we're not going at all. Now that I've found you, I'm not going to leave you alone."

She stared at him with tears in her eyes and said, "Thank you."

"Come on," he said, "I'll carry you if I have to."

He half-dragged, half-carried her to one of the windows and leaned her against the wall.

"Stay here."

He went back to the cot and picked up the blanket. The windows were made up of four small panes, so he would have to break not only the glass but also the wood between them. Hopefully, the blanket would muffle most of the noise.

Right at that moment there was a sudden clap of thunder, and the sky opened up.

The killer wasn't happy.

From where he was he could see the front of the building Clint Adams was in. If Adams went into the back room of that building he'd find the woman, the last "message" he meant to send Clint Adams. He hadn't killed her yet. He'd been planning to do it in such a way that Adams would really feel it. Now, if Adams found her, he'd untie her and . . . and what?

He thought about it for a minute. With the woman on his arm, weak from hunger and thirst just as he was, Adams would probably be hampered even more.

Yeah, this might work. He could hunt them both down and kill the woman right in front of him.

Yep, it might work at that.

Suddenly there was a clap of thunder, and it started to rain.

"Right on cue," Clint said.

"What?" the girl asked.

Clint looked at her and asked, "What's your name?"

"Robin," she said, "Robin Lee."

"Well, Robin," Clint said, "I'm going to punch out this window with the next clap of thunder, and hopefully our friend out there won't hear it."

She didn't say anything, just nodded and watched him with wide eyes. She still wasn't quite used to the idea that she was free—to some extent, anyway.

Clint stood in front of the window, both fists wrapped in the blanket, waiting for the next clap of thunder. When it came, he thrust his arms out convulsively. Wood splintered and glass broke, but as he had hoped, the blanket muffled it somewhat. He just hoped that the thunder covered whatever noise he *had* made.

"Come on," he said to Robin, reaching for her, "out you go."

The killer looked out at the rain. By now Adams would be trying to get out of the building through the back. Since there was no door, he and the girl would have to climb out a window.

The killer turned and picked up a rain slicker he had nearby. He was pleased with himself for having brought it. He had planned for almost every eventuality, rain being one of them. Not only would the slicker keep him dry, but his guns, as well.

He left the room to move to his next location.

Clint lifted Robin and pushed her out the window. Once she was outside, he handed her the blanket and told her to cover herself with it. The rain was coming down in unrelenting sheets. He hoisted himself up and climbed out the window head first. For a moment he thought he wasn't going to fit. He had to drop back into the room, remove his holster and hand it out to Robin. This time when he climbed out it was a tight fit, but with Robin tugging on one of his arms he finally fell to the ground outside.

He took the gun back as she tried to cover them both with the blanket. Apparently she'd managed to work some life back into her arms and legs.

"All right," he said as they huddled there together under the blanket, "now let's find someplace to wait out this rain."

They moved along behind the buildings, Clint's eyes flicking over them, looking for a likely shelter from the rain and from the killer. Suddenly he stopped. It was *so* sudden that Robin almost fell, and would have if he hadn't caught her.

"Sorry," he said, "I saw something back here."

It was almost dark now, as they backtracked about ten feet. There was an alley there, and in the alley, against the side of the building was a slanted doorway, which probably led to a root cellar.

"Here," he said, moving to the door. He reached for the handle and pulled the door open. Dust motes flew as he looked down at a stairway.

"Inside," he said.

"Are you sure?" she asked. Her look was doubtful as she studied the stairs.

"It's as good a place as any," he said. Finally she shrugged, gave him the blanket, and went down the steps. Clint followed, pulling the door closed behind them.

Now they were in total darkness.

The killer was upset.

Once again he had lost sight of Clint Adams. He had gotten caught up in the game-playing, leading Adams a merry chase, instead of killing him when he had the chance. It was time to stop carrying him and get it over with. He had other outlets for his vengeance. He didn't have to spend all his time on this one.

The driving rain had slowed him down, and by the time he'd reached the building across the street, Adams and the girl had gotten out through a window. He cursed himself for not having heard the glass break.

He stood outside the building, staring at the broken window, the rain washing down over him, running off his chin in a miniwaterfall.

This time when he found them—both of them—he would kill them for sure.

THIRTY-FOUR

"Hey?" she called, and it was then he realized that he hadn't told her his name.

"I'm here," he assured her. "My name is Clint Adams."

"Clint," she said, sounding like a little girl, "it's dark in here."

"We're underground," he said. "No windows."

"And no light."

"Wait," he said. He reached into his pocket, hoping he still had some lucifers and hoping they all hadn't gotten wet. He found one and gave it life with his thumbnail.

In the glow of the match he could see her standing very still, her shoulders hunched.

"Look around," he said. "See if there's anything here that will burn."

She nodded jerkily and started looking around.

"Well, well," he said.

"What?"

He walked to a lamp he had spotted and lifted it, hoping there was still some oil in it. He shook it and heard something shake inside.

"Will it burn?"

"Let's find out."

He hunched down, put it on the ground, and raised

the glass. He held the quickly dying match to the wick, which caught fire. Suddenly the room was almost light.

"That's better, isn't it?"

"It sure is," she said. She moved toward him and got down on her knees next to him. "I don't think I can stand any more."

"Stay here," he said.

"Where are you going?" she asked, panicked. Her hand closed convulsively over his sleeve.

"I'm just going to look around," he said. "I want to see if there's anything down here we can use. I can't go very far."

She smiled wanly, then used her hands to wipe the water from her face. Some of the dirt went with it, and he saw that she was even prettier than he had first thought she was.

He stood up and looked around them. The cellar had a dirt floor, but the walls had been reinforced with wood by someone who knew what he was doing when it came to carpentry. There were hooks on the walls, although nothing was hanging from them at the moment.

"I don't see anything," she said.

"Neither do I," he said, "but I'm going to take an even closer look."

The corners were still dark, and he had to walk right to them to see into them. In one corner he found a cot covered with a blanket.

"Well," he said, "we have a cot and a dry blanket."

"Good," she said, hugging her arms, "I'm cold."

"Here," he said, removing the blanket from the cot. "Get out of those wet clothes and wrap this around you." He shook the blanket out as much as he could, squinting against the dust, and tossed it to her.

She caught the blanket and stared at him.

"Get out of my clothes?"

"This is no time to be modest," he said. "You could catch your death of cold."

"Turn your back."

"I won't look," he said, but he lied. As he leaned over to look under the cot, he managed to catch just a glimpse of two small, hard, brown-tipped breasts as she wrapped the blanket around her naked form.

What he found underneath the cot, though, excited him much more than her nudity—under the circumstances.

There was a carton under the cot, and when he pulled it out he saw that it contained a canteen and some canned goods.

"Look what we have here," he said.

"What?"

He lifted the canteen and found that it was full.

"Water."

"Water?" she repeated anxiously. She stood up so abruptly that the blanket opened for a moment, revealing smooth thighs and a dark patch of hair. She gathered it back around her and moved to his side. "Water? Really?"

He unstopped the canteen and held it to his nose, then tipped it back to take a taste. It was warm and brackish, but it was wet.

"It's water, all right," he said. He handed her the canteen and said, "Take a couple of sips, and that's all. Understand?"

She nodded and grabbed the canteen from his hands. She took two swallows, then a quick third, as if she were stealing it.

Clint dipped into the carton and pulled out a couple of cans.

"Canned peaches," he said.

"Let's eat some," she said eagerly.

The peaches, and the sweet juice they were stored in, would go a long way toward building up their strength, he knew, but he also knew something else.

"We don't have anything to open them with," he said, and handed her one of the cans.

"You don't have a knife?" she asked.

"No."

She looked disappointed and he felt guilty, but only for a moment. After all, he was just as disappointed as she was.

"What do you suppose this stuff is doing down here?" she asked. "The blanket, the water, the food . . ."

"I don't know," Clint said. "I don't think the killer left it down here for us."

"The killer?"

"That's how I've come to think of him."

"Then if not him, who?"

"I don't know," he said. "One of the townspeople, I suppose. Maybe whoever it was feared some sort of attack, and stored this stuff down here just in case they needed to spend a few days here."

"Attack?"

"We don't know what made this a ghost town, Robin," he explained. "Maybe the town was attacked and the people were driven out. Who knows how long this stuff has been down here?"

"Judging from the water and the way it tastes, a long time."

Clint looked at Robin. That was the closest thing to a joke she had come to since they'd met.

"I agree," Clint said, "and that means that the killer doesn't know about this place."

"How do you figure that?"

"If he knew, he wouldn't have left all of this here. He would have moved it, used it for himself."

Robin pulled the blanket tightly around her with one hand and said, "It's too bad we don't know where he keeps his food."

"He probably has it cached all over town. He wouldn't want to hoard it all in one place, just in case I *did* manage to stumble across it."

Robin looked down at the can in her hand, then set it down.

"Well," she said, "these aren't much good to us without something to open them with, are they?"

"No, they're not." He stood up and brushed his hands together, knocking off the dirt from the floor. "That's why I'm going to go out and find something that we *can* open them with."

She stood up and took hold of his arm.

"You're going out?"

"I have to, Robin," he said. "We both need some nourishment."

"We have the water."

"We can't get by on that," he said. "I won't be gone long. I've just got to find something sharp to open the cans with." He put his hand over hers and said, "I'll be right back. I promise."

"I'm gonna hold you to that," she said.

THIRTY-FIVE

All he needed was a sharp piece of metal to puncture the can with. There was a knife in his saddlebags, but God only knew where they and Duke were. He realized with a start that he hadn't even thought about Duke for a long time. Where had the big gelding gotten to?

He'd been through enough of these old buildings that he must have seen a sharp hunk of metal somewhere. All he had to do was remember.

He left the root cellar carefully, closing the door softly behind him. It was very dark out. The rain had let up some but was still coming down. The clouds were hiding the moon. He'd be soaked to the skin by the time he got back. He wondered if Robin would share the blanket with him. He recalled the glimpse he'd gotten of her body, and scolded himself for thinking about that at a time like this. Still, she *was* pretty, and who knew if they'd come out of this alive?

Actually, that was no way to think, not when they had found themselves a place that the killer probably knew nothing about. He decided he'd pick up some dry wood to burn in the cellar. Just a small fire, to generate heat. Too big a fire and they would smoke themselves out.

He moved along behind the buildings, keeping close to the walls. He felt fairly certain that they had shaken the eyes of the killer. He was probably wondering right now where they were.

The rain was cold, but the wetness felt good on his face and lips. Now if he could only find something to open the cans with, they'd be able to get food inside of them.

The killer took to the rooftops to try to spot Adams and the girl. He spent an hour patrolling them, watching the streets, until he was completely soaked. It was too dark, he decided, for Adams to be out. He was probably holed up somewhere with the girl for the night. Yeah, well, let them enjoy the night and maybe even each other.

Tomorrow they would die.

Clint finally remembered an old hardware store he had been in. It was on this side of the street. When he reached it he was able to enter from the back. He did so slowly, carefully, until he was sure he was the only one in the building.

He moved from the back room to the main part of the store. He managed to find a burlap bag and filled it with small pieces of shelving. This wood would burn without much smoke. He also found a small basin, and realized that they could set it outside in the rain to catch some rainwater they could use to refill the canteen. He put that into the bag, also. He carried the bag to the back door and set it down there, then went back into the store to look for something to use as a can opener. Finally he realized what he might be able to use. If the shelves had been affixed to the walls with metal brackets, he might be able to find one sharp enough to use.

He sifted through the remnants of the shelving and finally found what he was looking for. It was an L-shaped bracket that tapered at one end. It might just be sharp enough to do the trick. He walked to the back door, put the bracket in the bag with the wood, then slung his booty over his shoulder and made his way back to the cellar.

"Who is it?" Robin demanded from the darkness as he entered.

"It's me."

She had turned the lamp down as low as it would go, and now turned it up again. The flame was flickering in prelude to going out. The oil was almost gone.

"What did you find?" she asked.

"Some wood for a small fire," he said, sticking his hand into the bag, "and this." He brandished the metal bracket as if it were made of gold.

"Will that work?"

"Let's try it."

They both went over to the cans of peaches. There were four cans, and Clint lifted one and positioned it between his knees. He lifted the bracket over his head and brought the tapered end down onto the top of the can. It made a dent but didn't puncture it.

"Try it again."

He'd had every intention of doing so, but he nodded to her, lifted the bracket, and brought it down again. A shower of juice shot up from a hole, and Robin actually cried out and clapped her hands, like a child who had found some precious gift beneath a Christmas tree.

He gave her the can, which she lifted to her lips. The nectar of the peach was very sweet and she drank deeply, then handed it to Clint. He finished it, relishing the flavor of it, then put the can back down and began to saw with the end of the bracket, until the hole in the can was big enough for him to get his fingers in to take out a peach. He gave the first one to Robin, then fished another out for himself.

"Oh, my God," she said, "I never tasted anything so good."

"I know," he said. There were two peach halves left in the can. He gave her one and ate the other.

"I found a basin that I've set outside to catch water," he said.

"Can we open another can?" she asked, licking her fingers.

"We'd better save them," he said. "I'm going to make a small fire, just for warmth."

He went to the burlap bag and upended it, dumping out the wood. He piled a few pieces in the center of the floor and went into his pocket for a lucifer.

"Last one," he said, taking it out. "Give me the lamp."

"What are you going to do?"

"Save this match as long as possible."

Actually, he was afraid that the last match was too wet to strike. Maybe if it dried out, they'd be able to use it tomorrow.

He took the lamp and removed the glass. The flame was almost out. He held a small piece of wood to it until it caught, then moved that flame to the wood on the floor. As the small fire caught, the flame in the lamp died.

"We're going to have to try to keep it going all night," he said.

"You didn't bring enough wood."

He looked around.

"The walls are wood," he said, "so we've got plenty. We'll be all right."

"You won't," she said.

"What?"

"Look at you," she said. "You're shivering."

It was only then that he noticed she was right: He *was* shivering.

"Get those clothes off," she said. "We can share the blanket."

He shucked his wet clothes and laid them alongside hers on the floor, near the small fire. She opened the blanket to him, and he moved next to her. It barely covered the two of them, but that wasn't where most of the warmth would come from. Most of it was going to come from their bodies, pressed together. For the moment, Clint's skin was cold, but as soon as his flesh touched hers, he felt her heat and began to warm up.

"Here," he said, putting one arm around her so they could get closer "put your head on my shoulder and try to get some sleep. I'll watch the fire."

"All right."

She put her head down and closed her eyes.

"Do you think we'll get out of here?"

"I think we're at least on even terms with him," Clint said. "We're armed, and he doesn't know where we are. I think we have a very good chance."

"You said you would tell me what this was all about."

He hesitated a moment, then said, "If I do, you might not want to share your blanket with me anymore."

She slid one warm arm around his waist and said, "Let's take the chance."

THIRTY-SIX

Clint explained to Robin that she had been an innocent victim, caught in a plot first to demoralize him, possibly drive him crazy, and then kill him.

He finished by saying, "I'm sorry you got caught up in all of this simply because you resemble someone . . . close to me."

She had her head on his shoulder the whole time, and now she lifted it and looked up at him. She put her hand on his chest, then pulled her hand away and gripped the edge of the blanket.

"It's not your fault."

"Whose fault is it?" he asked. "Three people are dead, and you would have been the fourth, just because you all looked like friends of mine."

"The fault is his," she said, "whoever he is."

"Whoever he is," Clint said. Wait a minute, he thought. "Robin, where did you meet him?"

"I was in a town called Whitten."

"Here in Oklahoma?"

"Yes. I was working as a waitress, and he came into the restaurant."

"This is important, Robin," he said. "What did he look like?"

"Tall, sandy-haired, young, in his early twenties, a little younger than me."

"Did you ever hear him say his name?"

She frowned, thinking back, then said, "No, he never told me that."

"Did you ever hear him talk to anyone else, anyone who might have called him by his name?"

"No," she said, shaking her head, "no one."

"How did he get you here?"

"He kidnapped me," she said. "I was walking home from work at night and he approached me from an alley. He asked me to go away with him, but I refused. I didn't like him. He-he scared me, even that first day when he came into the restaurant."

"Then what?"

"He grabbed me and knocked me out. The next thing I knew I was tied to a horse, and he brought me here."

"When was that?"

"That's difficult to say," she said. "I'm not really sure how long I've been here."

"Judging from your physical condition, it probably wasn't much longer than me. You might have been the last piece to the puzzle he was putting together for me."

"Don't you know who he is?" she asked.

"Not for sure," he said. "I think I might know, but . . ."

"Who?"

"I don't want to say until I'm sure," he said. "I'm fairly certain he's the son of someone I killed, many years ago."

"I know your reputation, Clint," she said, "but having met you, I can't believe any of it."

"Some of it is true," he said, "but not much. It all gets so exaggerated in newspapers and dime novels."

"Well, you saved my life," she said, "and I think you're a very gentle man."

"I won't be very gentle where he's concerned," Clint said. "Not after everything he's done."

She snuggled closer to him, and he threw a few more pieces of wood on the fire. In another hour or so he'd have to start tearing the walls apart for wood.

"Tomorrow," he said, "tomorrow this is all going to end. I promise you, and I promise myself."

"What happens if we die?" she asked.

"You won't die," he said. "If he kills me, he won't find you. You can come out after he leaves."

"I don't want him to kill you," she said. "Why can't we just slip away in the night?"

"With no horse?" he asked. "In our weakened condition we wouldn't get far."

"Oh, Clint . . ." she said, lifting her head from his shoulder again.

The rain had washed all the dirt from her face, which was very close to his now. He leaned down and kissed her, gently. Her mouth responded, and so did her body. She pressed herself more tightly against him, and he brought his hand up to cup one hard little breast.

"Oh, Clint . . ." she breathed again. "Tonight we're alive . . . I want to *feel* alive. . . ."

So they made love in the root cellar. What better way for a man and a woman to make each other feel alive?

He thumbed the nipple of her right breast as they kissed again, and she reached into his lap to find him hard and ready.

He spread the blanket on the floor, and they were

hardly aware of the coolness that touched their skin as they lay down together on it. He kissed her breasts, teasing the nipples with his teeth as his hand slid down over her belly and nestled between her legs, where it was incredibly wet and warm. Her hands came up to cup his head as he continued to nibble her breasts, and then he lifted one leg over her and straddled her.

"Yes," she said, "do it now, Clint, please. . . ."

He entered her slowly, and she was scalding. She caught her breath and let it out slowly as he slid into her inch by inch, and then when he was fully in her she lifted her legs and wrapped them around him. He slid his hands beneath her buttocks to cushion her, and then began to move in her, slowly at first, and then more rapidly. Her cries filled his ears, as did the pounding of his heart, and as they climaxed together they were more alive at that moment than any two people could have been. . . .

Later, they wrapped themselves in the blanket again and just sat together, not speaking until she broke the silence between them.

"Clint?"

"Hmm?"

"The woman I resemble," she said. "Is she very close to you?"

"We hardly see each other," he said. "But yeah, I'd say we were close."

"Do I truly resemble her?"

"No," he said, "not really. You have the same color hair, cut the same way, and the shape of your face is the same as hers. That's what probably caught the killer's eye—but no, you're not alike at all."

"Good."

"Why good?"

She pressed more tightly to him and said, "Because when you think of me—if you ever think of me—I want it to be *me* you're remembering, not her."

"Don't worry about that, Robin," he said, sliding his arm around her, "I'll always remember you."

THIRTY-SEVEN

When morning came there was a small section of one wall missing. Clint had to don his boots again and use the heels to kick the wall into pieces. Robin found it very funny for him to be standing there, naked except for his boots, kicking the wall.

Sunlight streaked through cracks around the door, and Clint gently woke Robin.

"We have to get dressed."

She pressed her head to his shoulder for one more moment and said, "I wish we could stay here forever."

"Come on," Clint said. "Today's the day."

"I know," she said. "I know."

They cast the blanket off and got dressed, their backs to each other despite the fact that they had been naked together all night. Sometimes watching a person dress was even more personal than seeing him or her naked.

Their clothes had not dried completely, but they couldn't afford to complain.

Clint opened another can of peaches, and they had them for breakfast. They took some sips from the canteen, and then Clint went outside to retrieve the basin of rainwater. He poured it into the canteen, filling it to the brim. They then shared what was left in the basin.

"All right," Clint said, "you've got to stay here."

"No."

"What?"

"I thought about it last night," she said. "I want to help."

"Robin, honey," he said, taking her by the shoulders, "believe me when I say the best way you can help me is to stay here, where I don't have to worry about you."

"But—"

"If I'm worrying about you," he said, "I might not be worrying enough about me. I could get killed."

She firmed her jaw, as if she were going to take a stand, but then relented. He could feel it in the slump of her shoulders.

"All right," she said, "but you have to promise to come back."

"I can't—"

"Promise!" she said, gripping both of his arms tightly, with surprising strength.

"Honey," he said, "I promise I'll do my best to come back. That's the best I can do."

She relaxed her hold on his arms and said, "All right, but I'm going to hold you to it."

"Robin," he said, "have I ever broken a promise to you?"

THIRTY-EIGHT

Fulton stopped just outside of Patience and stared down at the town from atop a rise. From here, the town looked dead, and even at this time of morning there should have been *some* kind of activity in the streets.

Patience was a ghost town.

Rick Hartman was right to worry about his friend. The only reason someone could have had for asking Clint Adams to meet him or her at a ghost town would be to set him up for something.

Fulton nudged his horse's ribs and started toward the town.

Clint had to figure out a way to draw the killer out. At this point he was fairly sure the man would not kill him from hiding. The man had to have enough confidence to face him on the street. Of course, he'd want to do it in his own time, but Clint didn't have any time left. Any second or third wind he might have found was waning very quickly. Without the proper nourishment he soon wouldn't even be able to pull the trigger on his gun.

He had to draw the man out . . . now!

The killer finished his breakfast and looked out the window at the main street. The rain had stopped halfway through the night, but the street was more mud puddle than anything else. It was time to go out and find Adams and the girl and get this over with.

He was about to move away from the window when he saw some movement out of the corner of his eye. He looked out the window again and couldn't believe what he saw.

Clint Adams was walking out into the middle of the muddy street, carrying a wooden chair. He set the chair down and then sat in it, folding his arms across his chest.

What the hell . . .

Clint didn't know whether this would work or not, but it was all he could think of. He was showing disdain for the man, almost daring him to come out and face him. Anyone who could set up something like this had to have an ego, and the only plan he could come up with was to tweak that ego and see what happened.

The killer intended to wait Adams out, but after twenty minutes of watching the man just sit there *he* was the one getting impatient.

He picked up a rifle and sighted down the barrel. He could have put a bullet right in Adams's head with no trouble at all.

He pulled the trigger.

The first bullet struck the muddy ground no more than three inches from Clint's left foot. Now he knew that the man could shoot. The second shot landed an inch away. Clint made a concerted effort not to move. He didn't even turn his head.

If this didn't tweak the man's ego, he didn't know what would.

●　●　●

Fulton had almost reached town when he heard the shots. He reined his horse in and dismounted. It would do no good to ride straight into a shootout. He slapped his horse on the rump, drew his gun, and started toward town on foot.

"Adams!"
Clint didn't answer.
"It's all over, Adams!" the killer shouted. "You get the next one right in the head!"
Clint still didn't answer, and he didn't move.
"Damn it, Adams! Say something!"
Finally Clint moved, just his head, so he could look up at the killer.
"Come on down!" he called out.

Fulton saw the man sitting in the chair in the middle of the street.
"What the hell . . ."

Before moving away from the window, the killer looked up and down the street. He saw a man on foot, holding a gun. He was across the street, and he was staring at Clint Adams. He had no idea that the killer was there.
The killer didn't know who the man was, or what he was doing there, but he had no time to fool with anyone else. He just aimed and fired, and dismissed him.

Fulton heard the shot and moved instinctively. He felt the sting of the bullet, and then he was falling. . . .

Robin Lee couldn't wait any longer.
After the first two shots she couldn't stand not know-

ing what was going on. She had opened the door a crack so she could listen, and now she pushed it open all the way and climbed out of the root cellar.

She worked her way down the alley until she reached the main street. To her left she could see Clint, sitting in a chair in the middle of the street. She heard the killer shouting and was able to pick out the window he was leaning out of. At that moment she saw the killer's rifle swing away from Clint, and the man fired. She looked to her right and saw a man spin at the impact of the bullet and go down.

She didn't understand what was going on, but she rushed toward the wounded man.

He wouldn't be using his gun.

THIRTY-NINE

Clint looked down the street and saw the man fall. He only caught a glimpse of him, but he thought he didn't know him. Just another innocent victim. Speaking of innocent victims, he saw Robin come out of the alley and run toward the fallen man.

Damn it, he'd told her to stay put.

He looked up at the killer's window, but he wasn't there anymore. He was probably—hopefully—on his way down to the street.

Clint's eyes felt raw, and he suddenly felt feverish again. The incidents of the next few moments would decide the whole matter, and he wasn't even sure he could stand up.

The killer hurried down to the street. It was time, he kept telling himself, time for revenge. It won't be long now, Pa, not long at all.

The killer appeared at the door, and Clint watched him set his rifle down and walk slowly out into the center of the street. His senses suddenly felt heightened. He could even hear the mud squishing beneath the man's boots.

"Adams," the man said.

Clint opened his mouth, hoping that his voice would work. His mouth felt dry.

"Wallmann, isn't it?"

The man looked surprised.

"You guessed."

"I figured it out, son," Clint said. The young man really did look a lot like his father, if Clint's memory was serving him well. "What's your first name?"

"Ken," the young killer said. "Ken Wallmann."

"Let's get it straight," Clint said. "Bill Wallmann was your father?"

"That's right," Wallmann said. "And you killed him."

"And now you're going to kill me?"

"That's right."

"Why all this other business?"

"Why? Because I wanted you to suffer first, that's why," the young man explained.

"Well, I did that," Clint said.

"Stand up."

Clint grinned wryly and said, "I'm not sure I can."

"Then I'll kill you while you sit," Wallmann said.

Clint put his hands on his knees to stand and knew immediately that he'd made a mistake. The young killer had been watching him closely and had chosen his moment well. Clint saw that he was going to draw his gun, and didn't think that he quite had the strength to draw his own.

Well, at least it would . . .

Robin knew something was wrong with Clint. She picked up the gun dropped by the wounded man, held it in both hands, pointed it at Ken Wallmann, and fired. . . .

• • •

Wallmann heard the shot and turned his head. The woman was holding the gun and fired again. She missed by a wide margin again, but he couldn't afford to give her another chance. She might get lucky.

He turned his gun toward her, preparing to fire.

Clint saw Wallmann turn toward Robin and saw her holding the gun. He hadn't even heard the shot or shots that she had fired. Obviously she had missed, but he knew Wallmann would not.

"No!" Clint shouted, standing up straight. His hand streaked for his gun and he shouted, "Wallmann!"

The young killer turned and looked at him, then started to bring his gun back around.

Instinct told Wallmann that after all of his careful planning he had just made his fatal mistake.

Clint fired, and the bullet struck Wallmann in the chest. The man staggered back but held on to his gun. He didn't fall, but righted himself and tried to bring his gun to bear on his enemy.

"Don't!" Clint shouted, but it was no use. He fired again, hitting Wallmann in the chest for a second time. This time Wallmann's gun fell from his fingers, and he fell down face first in the mud.

Clint reached behind himself for the chair for support. When he leaned on the back of it, one of the back legs sank into the mud. The chair tilted, and Clint fell. . . .

EPILOGUE

When Robin came out of the back room, Clint had some of the food he had found in Sam Fulton's saddlebags laid out. They were in the building Wallmann had last come out of, and could have had any of his supplies as well. There was nothing to stop them from eating and drinking as much as they wanted now. He had used the potbellied stove in the corner to heat up some bacon and beans and to make some coffee.

"How is he?" he asked Robin.

"He'll be all right," she said. "He said he heard the shot and moved in time. It struck him here," she said, touching herself just above the left hip, "and kept on going through. The bleeding has stopped."

"That's good."

"He won't be able to ride for a couple of days."

"Doesn't matter," Clint said. "We have enough supplies to last. We'll wait until he's ready, and then the three of us will leave."

She sat opposite him and looked down at the feast laid out in front of them.

After Wallmann had gone down, she had rushed to Clint, thinking he'd been shot. She held him up and they both checked Wallmann to make sure he was dead, and then went to help the man they later discovered was named Sam Fulton.

Together they had gotten Fulton bedded down on a cot in the back room, and Robin had patched him as well as she could.

"It looks good," she said. "I don't know where to start."

"Coffee," he said, handing her a cup.

"Um," she said, taking it and sipping. "Strong and good."

He raised his cup to her and said, "Just like you."

She smiled and picked up a plate of food.

While they ate she asked, "Were you right about who he was?"

"Yes," he said around a mouthful of hot food. "I'm sorry it had to happen this way. He'd been carrying a hatred of me around with him for a long time."

"Not only for you," she said. "He was angry all the time. I think he hated a lot of people."

"It fueled him," Clint said, "kept him going."

"In the end," she said, "it killed him, too."

"Yes," Clint said, "him and a lot of other people."

Robin reached over and laid her hand over Clint's.

"We'll bury them all before we go," she said, "even if I have to do it myself."

"Are you kidding?" he said, smiling. "After a feast like this we'll both be ready for anything."

She smiled at him and said, "Anything?"

He smiled back and said, "Yes, Robin . . . anything."

Fury knew something was wrong long before he saw the wagon train spread out, unmoving, across the plains in front of him.

From miles away, he had noticed the cloud of dust kicked up by the hooves of the mules and oxen pulling the wagons. Then he had seen that tan-colored pall stop and gradually be blown away by the ceaseless prairie wind.

It was the middle of the afternoon, much too early for a wagon train to be stopping for the day. Now, as Fury topped a small, grass-covered ridge and saw the motionless wagons about half a mile away, he wondered just what kind of damn fool was in charge of the train.

Stopping out in the open without even forming into a circle was like issuing an invitation to the Sioux, the Cheyenne, or the Pawnee. War parties roamed these plains all the time just looking for a situation as tempting as this one.

Fury reined in, leaned forward in his saddle, and thought about it. Nothing said he had to go help those pilgrims. They might not even want his help. But from the looks of things, they needed his help, whether they wanted it or not.

He heeled the rangy lineback dun into a trot toward

the wagons. As he approached, he saw figures scur-
rying back and forth around the canvas-topped vehi-
cles. Looked sort of like an anthill after someone
stomped it.

Fury pulled the dun to a stop about twenty feet from
the lead wagon. Near it a man was stretched out on
the ground with so many men and women gathered
around him that Fury could only catch a glimpse of
him through the crowd. When some of the men turned
to look at him, Fury said, "Howdy. Thought it looked
like you were having trouble."

"Damn right, mister," one of the pilgrims snapped.
"And if you're of a mind to give us more, I'd advise
against it."

Fury crossed his hands on the saddlehorn and shifted
in the saddle, easing his tired muscles. "I'm not looking
to cause trouble for anybody," he said mildly.

He supposed he might appear a little threatening
to a bunch of immigrants who until now had never
been any farther west than the Mississippi. Several
days had passed since his face had known the touch
of the razor, and his rough-hewn features could be
a little intimidating even without the beard stubble.
Besides that, he was well armed with a Colt's Third
Model Dragoon pistol holstered on his right hip, a
Bowie knife sheathed on his left, and a Sharps carbine
in the saddleboot under his right thigh. And he had
the look of a man who knew how to use all three
weapons.

A husky, broad-shouldered six-footer, John Fury's
height was apparent even on horseback. He wore a
broad-brimmed, flat-crowned black hat, a blue work
shirt, and fringed buckskin pants that were tucked into
high-topped black boots. As he swung down from the

saddle, a man's voice, husky with strain, called out, "Who's that? Who are you?"

The crowd parted, and Fury got a better look at the figure on the ground. It was obvious that he was the one who had spoken. There was blood on the man's face, and from the twisted look of him as he lay on the ground, he was busted up badly inside.

Fury let the dun's reins trail on the ground, confident that the horse wouldn't go anywhere. He walked over to the injured man and crouched beside him. "Name's John Fury," he said.

The man's breath hissed between his teeth, whether in pain or surprise Fury couldn't have said. "Fury? I heard of you."

Fury just nodded. Quite a few people reacted that way when they heard his name.

"I'm . . . Leander Crofton. Wagonmaster of . . . this here train." The man struggled to speak. He appeared to be in his fifties and had a short, grizzled beard and the leathery skin of a man who had spent nearly his whole life outdoors. His pale blue eyes were narrowed in a permanent squint.

"What happened to you?" Fury asked.

"It was a terrible accident— " began one of the men standing nearby, but he fell silent when Fury cast a hard glance at him. Fury had asked Crofton, and that was who he looked toward for the answer.

Crofton smiled a little, even though it cost him an effort. "Pulled a damn fool stunt," he said. "Horse nearly stepped on a rattler, and I let it rear up and get away from me. Never figured the critter'd spook so easy." The wagonmaster paused to draw a breath. The air rattled in his throat and chest. "Tossed me off and stomped all over me. Not the first time I been stepped on by a horse, but then a couple of the oxen pullin' the lead wagon got me, too, 'fore the driver could get 'em stopped.''

"God forgive me, I . . . I am so sorry." The words came in a tortured voice from a small man with dark curly hair and a beard. He was looking down at Crofton with lines of misery etched onto his face.

"Wasn't your fault, Leo," Crofton said. "Just . . . bad luck."

Fury had seen men before who had been trampled by horses. Crofton was in a bad way, and Fury could tell by the look in the man's eyes that Crofton was well aware of it. The wagonmaster's chances were pretty slim.

"Mind if I look you over?" Fury asked. Maybe he could do something to make Crofton's passing a little easier, anyway.

One of the other men spoke before Crofton had a chance to answer. "Are you a doctor, sir?" he asked.

Fury glanced up at him, saw a slender, middle-aged man with iron-gray hair. "No, but I've patched up quite a few hurt men in my time."

"Well, I am a doctor," the gray-haired man said. "And I'd appreciate it if you wouldn't try to move or examine Mr. Crofton. I've already done that, and I've given him some laudanum to ease the pain."

Fury nodded. He had been about to suggest a shot of whiskey, but the laudanum would probably work better.

Crofton's voice was already slower and more drowsy from the drug as he said, "Fury . . ."

"Right here."

"I got to be sure about something . . . You said your name was . . . John Fury."

"That's right."

"The same John Fury who . . . rode with Fremont and Kit Carson?"

"I know them," Fury said simply.

"And had a run-in with Cougar Johnson in Santa Fe?"

"Yes."

"Traded slugs with Hemp Collier in San Antone last year?"

"He started the fight, didn't give me much choice but to finish it."

"Thought so." Crofton's hand lifted and clutched weakly at Fury's sleeve. "You got to . . . make me a promise."

Fury didn't like the sound of that. Promises made to dying men usually led to a hell of a lot of trouble.

Crofton went on, "You got to give me . . . your word . . . that you'll take these folks through . . . to where they're goin'."

"I'm no wagonmaster," Fury said.

"You know the frontier," Crofton insisted. Anger gave him strength, made him rally enough to lift his head from the ground and glare at Fury. "You can get 'em through. I know you can."

"Don't excite him," warned the gray-haired doctor.

"Why the hell not?" Fury snapped, glancing up at the physician. He noticed now that the man had his arm around the shoulders of a pretty red-headed girl in her teens, probably his daughter. He went on, "What harm's it going to do?"

The girl exclaimed, "Oh! How can you be so . . . so callous?"

Crofton said, "Fury's just bein' practical, Carrie. He knows we got to . . . got to hash this out now. Only chance we'll get." He looked at Fury again. "I can't make you promise, but it . . . it'd sure set my mind at ease while I'm passin' over if I knew you'd take care of these folks."

Fury sighed. It was rare for him to promise anything to anybody. Giving your word was a quick way of getting in over your head in somebody else's problems. But Crofton was dying, and even though they had never crossed paths before, Fury recognized in the old man a fellow Westerner.

"All right," he said.

A little shudder ran through Crofton's battered body, and he rested his head back against the grassy ground. "Thanks," he said, the word gusting out of him along with a ragged breath.

"Where are you headed?" Fury figured the immigrants could tell him, but he wanted to hear the destination from Crofton.

"Colorado Territory . . . Folks figure to start 'em a town . . . somewhere on the South Platte. Won't be hard for you to find . . . a good place."

No, it wouldn't, Fury thought. No wagon train journey could be called easy, but at least this one wouldn't have to deal with crossing mountains, just prairie.

Prairie filled with savages and outlaws, that is.

A grim smile plucked at Fury's mouth as that thought crossed his mind. "Anything else you need to tell me?" he asked Crofton.

The wagonmaster shook his head and let his eyelids slide closed. "Nope. Figger I'll rest a spell now. We can talk again later."

"Sure," Fury said softly, knowing that in all likelihood, Leander Crofton would never wake up from this rest.

Less than a minute later, Crofton coughed suddenly,
a wracking sound. His head twisted to the side, and
blood welled for a few seconds from the corner of his
mouth. Fury heard some of the women in the crowd
cry out and turn away, and he suspected some of the
men did, too.

"Well, that's all," he said, straightening easily from
his kneeling position beside Crofton's body. He looked
at the doctor. The red-headed teenager had her face
pressed to the front of her father's shirt and her shoulders were shaking with sobs. She wasn't the only one
crying, and even the ones who were dry-eyed still
looked plenty grim.

"We'll have a funeral service as soon as a grave
is dug," said the doctor. "Then I suppose we'll be
moving on. You should know, Mr. . . . Fury, was it?
You should know that none of us will hold you to that
promise you made to Mr. Crofton."

Fury shrugged. "Didn't ask if you intended to or
not. I'm the one who made the promise. Reckon I'll
keep it."

He saw surprise on some of the faces watching
him. All of these travelers had probably figured him
for some sort of drifter. Well, that was fair enough.
Drifting was what he did best.

But that didn't mean he was a man who ignored
promises. He had given his word, and there was no
way he could back out now.

He met the startled stare of the doctor and went on,
"Who's the captain here? You?"

"No, I . . . You see, we hadn't gotten around to elect-
ing a captain yet. We only left Independence a couple
of weeks ago, and we were all happy with the leader-

ship of Mr. Crofton. We didn't see the need to select a captain."

Crofton should have insisted on it, Fury thought with a grimace. You never could tell when trouble would pop up. Crofton's body lying on the ground was grisly proof of that.

Fury looked around at the crowd. From the number of people standing there, he figured most of the wagons in the train were at least represented in this gathering. Lifting his voice, he said, "You all heard what Crofton asked me to do. I gave him my word I'd take over this wagon train and get it on through to Colorado Territory. Anybody got any objection to that?"

His gaze moved over the faces of the men and women who were standing and looking silently back at him. The silence was awkward and heavy. No one was objecting, but Fury could tell they weren't too happy with this unexpected turn of events.

Well, he thought, when he had rolled out of his soogans that morning, he hadn't expected to be in charge of a wagon train full of strangers before the day was over.

The gray-haired doctor was the first one to find his voice. "We can't speak for everyone on the train, Mr. Fury," he said. "But I don't know you, sir, and I have some reservations about turning over the welfare of my daughter and myself to a total stranger."

Several others in the crowd nodded in agreement with the sentiment expressed by the physician.

"Crofton knew me."

"He knew you have a reputation as some sort of gunman!"

Fury took a deep breath and wished to hell he had

come along after Crofton was already dead. Then he wouldn't be saddled with a pledge to take care of these people.

"I'm not wanted by the law," he said. "That's more than a lot of men out here on the frontier can say, especially those who have been here for as long as I have. Like I said, I'm not looking to cause trouble. I was riding along and minding my own business when I came across you people. There's too many of you for me to fight. You want to start out toward Colorado on your own, I can't stop you. But you're going to have to learn a hell of a lot in a hurry."

"What do you mean by that?"

Fury smiled grimly. "For one thing, if you stop spread out like this, you're making a target of yourselves for every Indian in these parts who wants a few fresh scalps for his lodge." He looked pointedly at the long red hair of the doctor's daughter. Carrie— that was what Crofton had called her, Fury remembered.

Her father paled a little, and another man said, "I didn't think there was any Indians this far east." Other murmurs of concern came from the crowd.

Fury knew he had gotten through to them. But before any of them had a chance to say that he should honor his promise to Crofton and take over, the sound of hoofbeats made him turn quickly.

A man was riding hard toward the wagon train from the west, leaning over the neck of his horse and urging it on to greater speed. The brim of his hat was blown back by the wind of his passage, and Fury saw anxious, dark brown features underneath it. The newcomer galloped up to the crowd gathered next to the lead wagon, hauled his lathered mount to a halt, and dropped lithely from the saddle. His eyes went wide with shock when he saw Crofton's body on the ground, and then his gaze flicked to Fury.

"You son of a bitch!" he howled.

And his hand darted toward the gun holstered on his hip.